The Old Dog's not Dead

Derek J. Byrne

Order this book online at www.trafford.com/
or email orders@trafford.com

Most Trafford titles are also available at major online book retailers.

Note for Librarians: A cataloguing record for this book is available from Library
and Archives Canada at www.collectionscanada.ca/amicus/index-e.html

Printed in Victoria, BC, Canada.

ISBN: 978-1-4251-8998-3 (soft)
ISBN: 978-1-4269-0057-0 (hard)

*Our mission is to efficiently provide the world's finest, most comprehensive
book publishing service, enabling every author to experience success.
To find out how to publish your book, your way, and have it available
worldwide, visit us online at www.trafford.com/10510*

Trafford rev. 8/11/2009

 www.trafford.com

North America & international
toll-free: 1 888 232 4444 (USA & Canada)
phone: 250 383 6864 ♦ fax: 812 355 4082

Acknowledgements:
I would like to thank my wife Anne for reading and improving the manuscript.

By the same author:

Past Echoes
Passage of Evil

Both Titles available from Trafford
Publishing (www.trafford.com)

CHAPTER 1

Peter Foster drove up to his house with a self-satisfied smile on his face. He was listening to the overture to the Marriage of Figaro on Classic FM. Classical music always lifted his spirits although they hardly needed lifting today. It was a sunny day and he had just finished a very satisfying lunch with his girlfriend. Unusually for him this relationship seemed to be going well. Peter felt he had met his soul mate in Peta. He knew he had told himself this before but this time, yes this time he really was sure he had found the genuine article. She was a private physiotherapist and as well as being physically attractive she was financially attractive as well. Not that that mattered to Peter; well not now anyway. As he parked the car at the front of his house he thought himself a lucky man. He got out and closed the car door without locking it. He always got a small tingle of satisfaction when he didn't lock his car or even his front door. It was one of the advantages of living out of the city. Another was being able to see the moon and stars so clearly at night. He was raised in the middle of a big city and always thought of himself as a city boy through and through. He used to think he couldn't survive without the stimulation of the city's noise and buzz. Petula Clark had called it "the rhythm of the traffic in the city" and Peter knew what she meant. But he had moved to the country and loved it. When he was starting off in life after leaving school at 16 years of age the city had given him a lifeline. He sold pirate videos and cassettes on the street and by working hard and being a reliable source of material he did well. Eventually he opened a small video store and went legit. One store become two and two became four. Things were really picking up for him. He had married Helen around that time and they had had a ball. He worked hard and played hard. For the first time in his life he had spare cash. They ate out at the best restaurants, entertained lavishly (by his standards anyway), and went on exotic holidays abroad. Life was great. He then added tanning studios to his video outlets and business got better and better. Everything he touched seemed to succeed. Failure was not in his vocabulary. He put all his success down to his hard work. Sure, Helen had supported him throughout as girlfriend and latterly, wife, and the tanning studios were her idea but the ultimate success was his baby. At school the teachers had told him that if he didn't pull his socks up, he would never amount to anything. What did they know? He was pulling up silk socks now. What were they doing? At school he was fairly popular. He was not good academically or at sport but he managed to charm the other pupils and most of them liked him. However his peers did vote him the pupil most likely to end up in prison. (This was an unofficial poll among the pupils and not one endorsed by the school). He did see their point. He had started off selling the dodgy videos and could easily have served time at Her Majesty's pleasure. But that was all past and now he was a pillar of the community. He was a member of the local golf club near where he lived and was a leading light in the local chamber of commerce. He had contributed to seminars on how to succeed in setting up and running a small business ("hard work; that's the answer in two words") and his advice and counsel was sought by many people. If he told himself the truth he was amazed by his own success even if on the outside he portrayed a self-confidence that boasted that his stature and success were his God-given right. He appreciated the fruits of his labours and knew he lived a privileged life. He had done what was necessary to get there because he couldn't go back to the situation of his childhood where money was tight and the family seemed to be always living on the edge of poverty. To him money was everything. He couldn't live without it; without lots of it.

CHAPTER 2

He sat at a table and stared at a notebook. He shook his head and then rubbed his forehead with his right hand. Sighing deeply he stood up and went over to the steaming kettle. He got a cloth and lifted the kettle off the gas flame using the cloth to protect his hand burning on the handle of the kettle which had long since lost its insulated covering. He then lowered the gas and replaced the kettle on the hob. Moving slowly he bent down to a cupboard and retrieved a teapot. He stood up and rubbed his chest. Maybe he should eat something before he left but he couldn't think of anything he fancied just then. He took the lid off the teapot and poured some boiling water in. This was swirled around so as to heat up the pot. He then poured the boiling water into the sink and placed two carefully measured teaspoons of tea into the pot. The pot was then half-filled with more boiling water and the lid replaced. The final act of preparation was the placing of a tea-cosy over the pot. He sat down again and felt tired. He was only up out of bed for an hour. How could he feel tired? He was getting old, he told himself. As he waited for the tea to draw he wondered if he should leave well alone. He wasn't a person who interfered much; he wasn't a nosy or gossipy neighbour. He took up the notebook and looked at it again. It was tatty and grubby but that was not surprising. As he flicked slowly through the pages he felt some small satisfaction at bringing this information to the notice of those who could make use of it. It was the visit he had made yesterday that had crystallized everything in his mind. He placed the notebook in a large brown envelope. He then folded the envelope over on itself and sealed it closed with sellotape. He felt his shirt pocket but seemed to draw a blank. He looked vaguely around the room. Why could you never find a pen when you wanted one? He'd have to get up again. He rose with difficulty and felt a little dizzy and had to hold onto the edge of the table to steady himself. As his head cleared he walked over to a drawer and opened it. He pushed the papers in it around but no pen was forthcoming. He now realized he'd have to go upstairs to his bedroom and get a pen from his jacket pocket. He decided to have a cup of tea first. He sat down again and with a slightly shaky hand poured himself a mug of tea. He added milk but no sugar. He picked up the newspaper and read the headlines on the front page. He was never an expert in current affairs but usually enjoyed browsing through the morning paper. This morning he couldn't muster up the interest or energy to read any of the articles. His arms felt so tired he didn't even try to turn the pages. These broadsheets were so awkward to manipulate but he could never bring himself to read a tabloid. Holding the paper seemed to exaggerate his shake and he was concerned about it, as he hadn't really noticed it being so bad before. He had always been afraid of becoming helpless as he got older. His father had had Parkinson's disease and it had broke his son's heart seeing how disabled and dependent his father became. It also scared him. He had always tried to keep fit. He was outdoors a lot in all weathers and was rarely found to be sitting and resting. That is until recently. He was getting old but up to now he had managed well. He cooked for himself and kept the place fairly tidy. He kept his mind active with crossword puzzles and taking daily walks kept him physically fit. He told himself he had the wee shake because he was tired. Then he worried about being tired. Why was he tired? He rubbed his chest again. He really should have something to eat with the cup of tea. He slowly finished the tea and drew the brown envelope towards him. He wouldn't need to address it as he intended to hand it over personally and explain the background to the details recorded inside. He saw the stub of a pencil on the top of his fridge. He could write the name on the envelope with that. That would do fine. He got up from the table very slowly this time. He still felt dizzy and then shaky all over. He got the pencil, sat down and carefully wrote a name on the brown envelope. After a few seconds thought he wrote the first line of the address. Well it was all ready now. He should set off and deliver it but he felt so tired. With the way he felt he thought he'd better stay in and forget about delivering his package that day. He could do it tomorrow. He'd go up and lie down now. He checked the back door was locked and left the kitchen to go upstairs. He stood at the end of the stairs and looked up. It may well have been the north face of the Eiger because he knew he wasn't going to be able to climb the stairs to his bedroom. He'd lie down on the couch and rest for a while. He opened the sitting room door and went over to the couch. He bent down to fix the cushions into a pillow for himself and as he did so he felt like he was falling down a black hole which looked bottomless. He knew he was dying. It was painless and he was almost relieved. He wouldn't end up helpless and bedridden. That was his last thought and it made him die with the slightest smile on his face.

CHAPTER 3

To be honest the days were long. He felt like staying in bed all day but he forced himself to get up at 10 every morning. He put in the time with great difficulty. He had his rules though. No television before 6pm and no alcohol before 10pm either at home or in a pub. Smoking was his main pleasure. He had been hounded by his wife and daughter to stop smoking because it would kill him. He grimaced at the irony that they had both passed away and he was still on the go. He had no immediate family as he had drifted away from his brother and sisters over the years. His only friends were his drinking buddies in the pub who he met most nights for an hour. They were dwindling in numbers as year after year more of them fell off the perch. He got up at 10 as usual and got his breakfast; tea and toast and marmalade. The same as yesterday and the day before and the day before that and so on. He then washed and shaved. After that he had a short wander around the back garden. God, it was out of hand. He used to love it but as he got older it got bigger and bigger. The plants that were tended to so carefully by his wife so many years ago were now running wild. He looked at the apple tree they had bought and planted and looked after thinking it would never grow and bear fruit. They had been so impatient. Now it was twelve feet tall and nearly as wide. Most of the apples were inaccessible and were rotten when he found them on the ground. The impatience had now turned to resignation. He was waiting to die. He knew this himself and was not frightened by it. He would never consider suicide. He had made that decision after his daughter died and he had found her body tucked up in bed in her apartment. He knew then his life was over. He was just marking time now. This was in stark contrast to the enthusiasm he had had for life when he first retired. His colleagues used to tell him that his retirement would be a great loss to them as he was so active and such an asset with all his experience. He had appreciated such comments and at the time had let himself believe them. Of course he knew that the place would function perfectly well without him. He had returned within two months of leaving and was not recognized by the man at the reception desk who was new. This shocked him and although his old comrades were soon hugging him and chatting to him nineteen to the dozen he still felt the chill of the outsider. He never returned but some of his former colleagues did call to his home occasionally, although not for a long time. He came in from the garden and sat down and made himself a list of things to do that day. He had started this after his daughter died. He knew the list was silly but he could not stop making one every morning. Everything was put on it: having meals, going to the shops, washing his clothes. He seemed to need the list to give his life structure and purpose. It was a red letter day if the car tax needed to be paid or the television license renewed. On those days the list had a sensible item on it. Sadly today was not one of those days. It was the shopping, the laundry and the hoovering. The shopping was done for a single meal at a time. That meant twice a day: once for lunch and once for tea. As breakfast was always tea and toast and marmalade, supplies of these items were always available. The two shopping trips killed more time. Anyway walking around the supermarket was reassuring. There were people there and the noise of them talking to each other was comforting. It counteracted the loneliness and silence of the house. Occasionally he would meet a neighbour and they would exchange pleasantries about the weather or the price of eggs or whatever. He now liked talking to people. When he was younger and had his wife and daughter at home he wasn't a great talker. He would prefer to read the paper or listen to the radio and relax. He used to find making conversation a bit stressful. It meant thinking of things to say or thinking of appropriate answers or reactions to the topic under discussion. The "wrong" answer or reaction would spark off a "can you get your nose out of that paper just for one minute" or "no, you listen to your football; don't mind me". So he had slowly tried to retreat from conversation with his family, with some success. Now that they were gone he craved for some social intercourse. When he worked, he had dedicated himself to his job and had slaved away for long hours above and beyond the call of duty. As a result he had no hobbies and now that he was retired he regretted this but seemed unable to push himself to take up a new pastime. He used to admit to himself reluctantly that supermarket shopping was his only pastime. That embarrassed him. His cronies in the pub used to travel all over the country using their pensioners' free travel privilege. It sounded interesting but it wasn't for him. If they invited him he would make up some excuse that he was too busy to go. It was a contradiction. He wanted human contact but he didn't want to get too close. The supermarket chats were ideal. It was like using a prostitute for sex rather than having an affair: not that he had ever done either. With these thoughts in his head he left the house for the supermarket.

CHAPTER 4

He had been found by a neighbour who had had a key for his house for many years without ever having the need to use it. However he had not seen Mr. Sims for two days and that was unusual. He had gone to the front door and rang the bell a few times. He had then gone around to the back door and knocked loudly. There was no answer. He wondered what to do. He went back to talk to his wife to see what she thought.

"We have a key. Remember he gave it to us that time he went to Lourdes for a week. We never gave it back".

"Oh yeah. But I wouldn't like to go in just in case .... well ...... you know ......"

"But if something has happened to him, if he is lying injured on the floor, we may save his life by going in. I'm sure he wouldn't mind."

"OK. But you come with me"

She looked at her husband as you would look at an errant child, sighed and said

"I'll get the key".

They went through the front gate both wanting to hang back and not be the first to the door.

"We had better ring the bell again, just in case ...."

He rang the bell three times hoping against hope to get an answer; trying to put off (what seemed now to be) the inevitable entry to the house.

"Maybe he's gone on a short holiday."

"We need to go in. Now let's do it."

She handed him the key and he opened the door gingerly.

"Mr. Sims, Mr. Sims. It's Jerry and Elaine from next door. Are you OK?"

They went into the kitchen and saw a cup with some tea in the end of it.

"He's not here" said Jerry stating the obvious. Elaine threw her eyes up to heaven.

"We'll try upstairs next."

"What about the sitting room? The door is ajar."

Jerry hesitated. Elaine pushed past him and opened the door fully. The room in front of her was clear but when she looked around the door she saw the body lying on the floor. She drew back suddenly and bumped into Jerry coming in the door.

"He dead" she said succinctly.

"I'll call the ambulance" Jerry said quickly, using it as an excuse not to view the body. He hesitated as he put his mobile to his ear.

"Are you sure he's dead?"

"I may not be Quincy, but yes, I'm sure he's dead."

The ambulance came but he was taken straight to the hospital morgue. He had been dead for at least 24 hours according to the paramedic who seemed to Elaine a bit of a know-it-all.

It was a Coroner's case and a post-mortem was performed. The cause of death was given as acute myocardial infarction secondary to coronary artery thrombosis. Elaine and Jerry had to attend an inquest and give their evidence of finding the body.

"I wonder how quickly they'll sell the house" Elaine whispered to Jerry as they left the inquest.

"Ah stop; you're terrible. Anyway it's none of our business."

"I bet you that son from Canada will inherit everything. And he never paid his father much heed. He'll be over hotfoot now. You can bet your bottom dollar (Canadian, of course) on that."

Jerry laughed.

"You're terrible" he concluded again.

As predicted two days later Paul arrived from Canada with wife and two children in tow. They called into Jerry and Elaine to ask them some details of finding the body. The questions were asked in a suspicious way and Jerry and Elaine both felt uncomfortable as if they were suspected of doing something improper. As they were leaving Jerry said that if they needed anything just to pop in. Paul looked at him as if he had two heads.

"We're not staying in that pokey place. Miriam would never stand for it."

"Oh" was all Jerry could muster.

"We're staying in the Grand in town. Will you be going to the funeral?"

Jerry said they would. Paul turned and walked down the drive to his car. Jerry went back into *his* pokey house and closed the door.

There wasn't many at the funeral. Obviously Paul and Co., were the chief mourners. A few of the neighbours also attended. They spoke to Paul at the end of the service and made the usual noises.

"Lovely man."

"A real gentleman."

"A great gardener."

"One of a kind."

Paul and Miriam (they didn't bring the children – too morbid) shook hands with everybody and smiled in a suitably somber way. There was no wake. Elaine talked of tight-fisted and snobby. Jerry called her terrible.

CHAPTER 5

Marlene Milroy finished her lunch. She looked at her watch. She'd have time for a smoke and still be in time for her shift. She didn't like back shifts. You got home just in time for bed. It gave your social life a right knock on the head. Still you got a long-lie in the morning. Swings and roundabouts and all that. She asked Liz to accompany her for a cigarette. They both went to the designated smoking area which the hospital provided - with some reluctance, Marlene thought. She often thought the reason all the smokers were made to gather in one place was to give the hospital easy access to carry out a mass execution of the smokers if and when they thought they could get away with it.

She made it to the ward in time for the handover. Thankfully the ward was quiet. Her shift passed reasonably quickly. She gave a handover at 10 o'clock and was leaving by the front door of the hospital by 10.30. Her phone rang as she was walking down the steps. An old man gave her a rather withering stare. It gave Marlene a shiver down her spine. This was soon forgotten as Dave her boyfriend was on the other end of the phone.

"I thought you should be finished by now. Am I right?"

"Yes I'm all done here. What's you up to?"

"Hoping to see you."

"I'm very tired. I'm on an early tomorrow so I think I'll go straight to bed."

"Don't let me stop you. I won't get in the way if I come over. Know what I mean?"

"Unfortunately, yes I do. But we both know where that will lead. Been there. Done that. I am now an older and more experienced lady and I want to be up bright and busy in the morning."

"That's a no then?"

"Yes, it's a no."

"Are you sure it's not no, it's a yes?"

"No. I'm sure it's a no, I think. You're messin' with my head as usual."

Marlene smiled to herself. She knew she was weakening and she knew that Dave knew she was weakening.

"Look, all jokin' aside I need to get a good night's rest. So much an' all as I'd like to see you I will deprive myself of the pleasure of your company until tomorrow. OK?"

"Oh my aching heart. How will I hold out until tomorrow. I suppose I'll have to go to the pub and drown my sorrows. The demon drink is all I have left in my sad life."

"Ring me tomorrow. Goodbye you saddo."

Marlene ended the call with a smile on her face. She was proud of herself that she hadn't given in to his charm. How many nights had she partied and went to work with little or no sleep? It was fun but now she was a senior staff nurse looking for a charge nurse post and she couldn't go to work hung over. She felt she was definitely maturing but hoped she wasn't turning into an old fuddy-duddy. No, that was a long way off, wasn't it?

She arrived at her car with these thoughts running through her head. She had been able to park near the main entrance when she had arrived at lunchtime which now saved her a long walk in the dark to the large car park at the other end of the hospital grounds.

She drove the short journey to her waterfront apartment. She had paid more than she could afford for the property but she loved it so much she had decided to stretch herself to get it. She had taken on agency work to make ends meet and had been working all the hours God sent. But she hadn't regretted it. She was devastated when it flooded due to a burst pipe a few years ago. She was amazed at how much damage a burst pipe could cause. She had had to move out for two weeks and stay with her friend's boyfriend. She was relieved when she moved back and the place was as good as new. It was like a family member recovering from a serious illness.

She flopped down on the couch when she came in. She resisted the allure of a glass of red wine.

'Maybe I am becoming an old fuddy-duddy' she thought. Still she was happy she could resist the temptation. She made herself a cup of tea and toasted a muffin. She piled the butter on the muffin letting it melt in before she sat down and tucked in to her supper as she watched Champions league highlights on the television. Arsenal won. Sleep would come easy that night.

CHAPTER 6

He was unpacking his few purchases which would make up his lunch when he heard the doorbell ring. He immediately felt tense. Who could it be? He hoped it wasn't the local minister trying to lure him back to religion. He'd seen him doing his rounds last week but so far he hadn't had a visit. Maybe this was the day. After his daughter died he had given up organized religion. He still believed in God but did God really want all the rules and ceremony that surrounded most religions. He didn't think so and had stopped attending church on Sundays. He missed some of the social contact but as he respected the beliefs of the rest of the congregation he couldn't attend the services without some commitment and faith. He did not want to be a hypocrite – they got a bad press in the Bible. He tried to look out the front room window to see if he could identify who was at the door. It was Bill. That was great. He nearly broke through the wall trying to get to the front door before Bill got away.

"Bill, welcome. Come on in."

"Greg, how are you? Thanks."

Bill came in. Greg was positively beaming at him. He was like a long lost son, just returned.

"How is the man? Enjoying his retirement?"

"What do you think Bill?" he said, not wishing to lie and not daring to speak the truth.

"Long time, no see. What are you up to anyway?"

"Oh this and that. You know me always on the go."

"You sure were. We still miss you at the station. All the boys passed on their regards when they heard I was visiting you. All that are left anyway. How long are you retired now?"

"Just over three years. In some ways it feels like yesterday and in another way it seems like I never worked at all. How are all the guys anyway?"

"Jinkie has retired. He went early due to his chest. He's still coughing like an old nag or was when he left. I must call in on him too. Little Pete died, but I suppose you heard that." Greg nodded.

"I need to see his widow. I've been meaning to do that for months."

"You should have been a social worker. You're wasted doing police work. How's Terry. Did he ever come back after the surgery?"

"Oh yeah. As big and bold as ever. Still thinks he's the best thing since sliced bread. I wouldn't wish him bad but a lot of people were hoping he wouldn't come back. Anyway it's hard to get rid of a bad thing, I suppose."

"I must pop in and see all the lads. I miss them but you

know how things are. Once you're gone you do feel a bit of an outsider."

"Not you surely. You are part of the bricks and mortar of the place. You'd never be an outsider there. Come down next week and you'll get a great welcome."

Greg smiled as if consenting but he knew he wasn't visiting the station again. He was not part of that life anymore and he wasn't one to pretend.

"Have you taken up golf or anything?"

"No, I never really liked it. It's one way to ruin a good walk. I'm happy enough" he lied.

"Anyway, the reason I came was to deliver a package. I don't know what's in it but I need to tell you some background before I give it to you."

Greg's eyes twinkled when he heard about the package like a faithful dog when he hears his master's key in the door. Bill noticed the change and inwardly felt sad. He could see that Greg was fading away. He had been shocked when Greg had opened the door. But what could he do? Call in more often perhaps.

"Who is the package from?"

"Let me fill you in. It was found when we searched the house of a man who was found dead in his sitting room by his neighbours. The ...."

"Was there foul play involved?"

"Always the policeman, eh Greg? No he died of natural causes, a heart attack I think. Anyway when his house was searched this package was found with your name and the address of the station on it. It was sealed so we obviously didn't open it."

"What was the dead man's name?"

"Frederick Sims. Did you know him?"

"No, I don't think so. The name means nothing to me. Did he have a record or anything?"

"Not that we found. His neighbours said he kept himself to himself."

Greg could identify with that.

"Where did he live?"

"Cottonside Road. You know it?"

"Yeah, sure. Still means nothing to me."

"Anyway I'll need to get going. Here's the package. So you'll call in next week to the station, yeah?

"I'll try."

Greg turned the package over gingerly in his hands as he showed Bill to the door. The two old comrades shook hands and said goodbye.

CHAPTER 7

Peter Foster sat on his patio sipping a glass of Chianti. He loved Italian red wine and drunk nothing else. He was listening to Richard Tauber singing from Offenbach's Tales of Hoffman. The sun shone on his face and he reflected again on his good fortune. He did really appreciate his life style, all the more because it was in stark contrast to his early life. Money was always tight as his father drank most of it. He always resented his father and craved for a father figure in his life. He pitied his mother as she thought that her only role in life was keeping her husband happy. There was no physical violence from husband to wife but a psychological war constantly raged, with his mother always on the losing side. As a result of this he lost interest in family life. The only thing he could thank his father for was inheriting his love of classical music. His father would play the music loudly when he came home drunk, conducting the orchestra with an imaginary baton in front of the record player. At those times Peter never wanted the music to stop because when it stopped his father would start ranting and raving and throwing things. To Peter, classical music meant peace and calm even if it was the calm before the storm. School could have been an escape from this misery but he did not like school and was in constant trouble there. He never saw the advantage of reading Shakespeare or knowing that the Battle of Hastings took place in 1066 or that one of Bolivia's main exports was tin. Because he was not interested he was disruptive and he was never short of volunteers to join in his schemes. Many of these centered on "mitching" from school and going to the cinema or an amusement arcade or somewhere else. On one occasion he smuggled alcohol into the geography class and drank it with one of the other trouble makers. Looking back now it all seemed a bit silly but he would quite happily defend himself to his ex-teachers and say "Look I've done well without any academic success. School isn't for everyone." However he'd be the first to admit he'd had some good breaks. When he had started selling some pirate music cassette tapes he met Charlie Osgood who described himself as an importer/exporter. He had advised Peter to get into video tapes. He could supply them if Peter could distribute them. Peter was doubtful. Not many people had video cassette players but Charlie was convincing and Peter took his advice. Over the next few years Charlie and himself did a huge amount of business together. Charlie was a bit of a loner but seemed to want to take Peter under his wing. Peter had found his father figure. However their businesses were entirely separate and Peter got no financial support from Charlie.

"To succeed in business you need to know you can stand on your own two feet. You need to have that confidence."

Peter did get that confidence. He thrived. He was also lucky (at least at that time) in marrying Helen. She had been a huge driving force in going legit and in developing the video business and tagging on the tanning salons which were a huge money earner. Charlie was delighted to see him succeed so well and there was certainly a tinge of fatherly pride in his delight. Charlie himself was hugely successful in business. Peter was never entirely sure of the exact way that Charlie made his money and he didn't pry.

On one occasion while talking late into the night over a bottle of whiskey Charlie got a bit maudlin. He expressed regret at never having a child and refusing his wife's desire to adopt. She was now dead and he felt alone in the world.

"You're the nearest thing I have to a relative" he said to Peter, much to Peter's embarrassment.

"Well I'll always be here for you Charlie. You know that."

"I sure do" Charlie replied, throwing his arm around Peter in drunken camaraderie.

"I've never lent you a penny. We both know that and we both know the reasons for that. You have made it without any financial help from me. You're your own man. But I've left you everything in my will. I didn't mean to tell you. But I want you to know how much I think of you. I love you like a son."

Tears ran down Charlie's face and Peter felt uncomfortable. He wasn't good at emotion. He mumbled something about not wanting Charlie's money and Charlie then changed the subject. They talked about this and that. Charlie asked how Peter was getting on with his new girlfriend.

"Very well actually. We're taking it slowly. She's a very independent woman."

"What's her name again? I know it's like yours. Is it Petra?"

"No. It's Peta. You were nearly right."

"Well I hope you have found true love and happiness. You had enough trouble with your divorce from Helen."

Peter didn't need reminding of that. It had been an emotional wringer. But Charlie was always there for moral and emotional support. When things went pear shaped with Helen he had been a very calming influence for Peter.

"You'll get screwed. Take it on the chin and start again. You've made a fortune once. Now do it again."

Peter tried to be as philosophical as Charlie but found it hard. Charlie was right. He would be screwed for every penny, and he probably deserved it. He had started playing around, while she had been faithful and a paragon of virtue. He didn't know why he had gone with other women. It sounded like a cliché and he used to smirk and feel embarrassed when he heard other men saying it, but the other women *really* didn't mean anything to him. He still loved Helen but she seemed to be distant. There was much less cuddling and kissing and even though they had sex regularly enough, he felt Helen couldn't have cared less. It was not something you could put your finger on; not something you could record as an incident that took place at a particular time and place. It was something that was hard to put into words. His affairs seemed unreasonable and he was certain a divorce court would see them in that light. Helen did not appear to have done anything to justify him running off into the arms of another (and another and another). He didn't contest the divorce and in his usual money-saving fashion represented himself at the divorce negotiations. This was against all the advice he got. He felt he didn't need any of those vulture solicitors. As predicted he got screwed. He had to sell the business to settle the alimony. The house would have to be next. He was now short of money for the first time in years. He could go to Charlie and ask for a loan but he knew he would be refused and he didn't want to put Charlie in the difficult position of refusing a loan. The bank was unlikely to accept a loan application as his business was now defunct. What were his alternatives?

CHAPTER 8

Greg walked back into the living room and put the parcel on the table. It was addressed to him at the police station where he used to work. It was written in pencil by a shaky hand. He didn't recognize the name of the person it was from. For some reason he was not anxious to open it. He felt an unjustified anxiety when he looked at the parcel. He couldn't explain it. It seemed that even though his life was boring he did not want any incident to upset the routine. He constantly thought to himself that he would welcome some excitement in his life but when a candidate for this excitement came along he was not happy to grab it. He didn't understand himself. He was angry and confused and frustrated. He knew he would have to open the parcel sooner or later but he decided to make a cup of tea first. He felt tears in the back of his eyes as he went to put on the kettle. He used to be so proactive, so inventive and so brave. He had had awards for bravery in the line of duty as well as for initiatives in the work place. Most of his peers respected him and those that didn't were jealous of him and his achievements. Now he was afraid to open a parcel. He would be better off dead. He was dead to all intents and purposes. He felt he was nothing. Why did he have to get old and so useless to himself and everyone else? He recalled the days when he was the man that his colleagues came to for advice. Any problem that they were faced with was put before him and he would come up with a solution. One of the proudest days he could remember was when he was summoned to see the Chief Constable. Before the meeting he was worried that some complaint had been received about him. In those days complaints were not very prevalent and it was usually a serious matter if a complaint was received. He couldn't recall any reason why there should be such a problem. Even so he was anxious as he waited outside the office. All his anxiety was misplaced. The Chief Constable had had a difficult problem related to a local councilor and a prostitute. He had asked Greg how he would handle such a situation as he had had similar situations in the past. He had given his advice which was followed and the whole situation was sorted out quietly and easily. He had had a discreet phone call after that to thank him for his sound advice. Even though the whole episode was confidential, certain mumblings and murmurings had filtered down. After that an invincible aura had surrounded him.

Even the people he had arrested over the years had had some respect for him. He treated everyone fairly and was straightforward and easy to deal with. Confidence oozed from him. How had he lost it all in the matter of a few years? Certainly the passing away of his wife and daughter hadn't helped. Their deaths, especially that of his daughter, had given his confidence a kick in the face. He had been unable to help them or to stop them dying. He had always been able to control a situation and to affect the outcome. With death he now felt that was impossible. In his head he had always known (like everyone else) that death could not be cheated. But now he knew it in his heart and that had hit him hard. He now went from day to day waiting for his own death. He knew there was no point in fighting it. He didn't give up smoking or alcohol. He ate a poor diet. He got little or no exercise. Who cared? Not him. His eyes wandered back to the package. Frederick Sims: he thought about the name over again. No he definitely didn't recognize it. The thought had gone through his head that he may have been sent a device that would injure him. Was Sims someone he had arrested and this was his final revenge from beyond the grave? He didn't think so. These things were racing through his head as he made a cup of tea. He drank it slowly putting off opening the parcel for as long as possible. He finished the tea and washed the cup slowly. He could ask the guys at the station to check with the computer. That seemed to be able to tell them everything. He had never got to grips with it: old dogs and new tricks and all that. But computers seemed to be ruling the roost so maybe he could make use of them now. But that might open a bigger can of worms. What if the parcel contained something to sully his good name? What could that be? He wasn't a saint but he couldn't recall any incident that could be brought up now and bring shame on him. Then why was he afraid ..... yes, afraid of the parcel?

"My God, what a miserable wimp I've become" he muttered to himself and felt like crying.

With that he marched over to the parcel, picked it up and ripped it open.

CHAPTER 9

Peter had been forced into a corner. He had been given a low level job by an acquaintance but he got the clear message that it would just be a temporary arrangement and a short temporary arrangement at that. He thought about asking Charlie for help. He was living in Scotland now: in the back of beyond somewhere. Peter wanted to be around the city so as to try and get back on track again as quickly as possible. His acquaintance, who was a surveyor, suggested that he should look for a proper job.

"You know 9 to 5 and all that."

"But I am not qualified to do much except to work as a manager in the retail sector. But that means working your butt off to make lots of money for someone else. I know this because up until recently I was that someone else."

No, he'd have to set himself up in business. He knew the banks wouldn't entertain him. He had nowhere else to turn. He went to see someone who was recommended to him by the friend of a friend. This someone seemed like a very pleasant and reasonable chap.

"Not a problem at all Mr. Foster. We can manage that."

Peter was satisfied with his business-like tone. His enterprise seemed to be efficient and well run. The interest rate could have been better but he was in no position to negotiate. He was very relieved now that it was done and dusted and he had borrowed the money: a lot of money.

Peta was just getting started in setting up her physiotherapy clinic and Peter played down his difficulties in case he would frighten her away. Anyway he would never borrow from her.

He had spoken to Charlie and they had decided that video tapes and shops were passé. People were getting lazier and never wanted to move off the couch. The masses desired spoon feeding. Their idea (mainly Charlie's) was to set up a mail order DVD rental service. You paid a flat monthly rate and for that you could hire as many or as few DVDs as you wished. There was no deadline for sending them back. The flat monthly rate meant guaranteed monthly income. It all sounded wonderful. He would make another fortune.

Over the next few months he spent all his waking hours setting up the business. He had to organize a premises and the DVD supply first. Then there was the initial mail shot and advertising campaign. At least with a shop, people could see it as they passed by and it basically advertised itself. With a mail order business you had to tell people you were around and explain the service you were providing. As it was a new idea it needed a hard sell. Charlie gave him the name of someone to assist in publicizing the business. He seemed to know what he was doing but charged very steeply. When Peter had

casually mentioned this to Charlie he had been told in no un-
certain terms that the normal fee for such services would be
about ten times what he was being charged. Reluctantly Peter felt grateful. Overall setting things up did not seem to be
as easy as the last time. He knew he should be patient. Rome
wasn't built in a day and all that. But he felt he had already
built Rome and that Helen had knocked it down. He wanted
it back instantly.

After a few weeks the mail shot was ready. This was com-
bined with an advertisement campaign in newspapers, popular magazines and commercial radio. According to Charlie's
contact television would have been better but when Peter
heard the price he baulked and went with the radio campaign.
The plan was an intense short exposure for two weeks to be
followed up a month later by another week of exposure. Peter felt he was opening himself up to great financial risk by
putting all this money up front but without the publicity the
business would never get going. Once the advertizing started
Peter employed three people to run the show. He would be
in direct control for the moment but when things took off he
would appoint a manager and he would start back into the
good life. Again more outlay, but he knew once people started
ordering DVDs he would have to be able to respond quickly
and efficiently if he was to have any hope of making it. A few
happy customers and the good news would spread by word of
mouth.

Applications to join started to come in quickly once the
advertising campaign started. Peter began to relax. Maybe
all the outlay would be worthwhile. Maybe the good life was
back.

CHAPTER 10

After ripping off the wrapping he pulled the contents out. It was a well used and rather grubby spiral bound note book. He turned it over to view the front cover. It said "Gardener's Notes 2000". What the hell was this? There must have been some mistake. He had no real interest in the garden. That was his wife's forte. Maybe the book was meant for her. But no, she was 10 years dead. That couldn't be right. He opened the first page.

Jan 6: Crepis rubra and Nigella damsascena planted by far rockery. Remember to look at patch of front lawn tomorrow.

Jan11: Will need to get turf for front lawn patch. Cleared out glass house and sprayed with Jeyes fluid and washed floor with same.

He flicked on a few pages.

Feb 28: Heater overhauled. Working fine. Melon seeds planted. Tomatoes put in as well. Slightly late this year. Begonia tubers set into potting mix. They were superb last year. Hoping for the best again.

He felt a rising tension borne of uncertainty of what was going on. He went to the centre of the book.

June 19: Lilies flowering better than last year. Very crowded though. Will split them in the Autumn. Cosmos very spindly this year. ?too little feeding ?not enough sun. Will up feed next year.

He went to end of the book.

Dec 20: Sprouts will be perfect for Christmas. Planting them that bit earlier definitely made a difference.

What was this? He threw it aside. Some dead bloke had put this in an envelope and addressed it to him at the station. Well, they weren't going to make a monkey out of him. Could it be the lads at the station? He doubted it. The new ones didn't know him and the old ones respected him too much. Bill would never be party to something like that. Who was this old guy anyway? He couldn't remember his name: Simons or Simmons. He'd need to contact Bill and ask him the name and see if could work out any contact that he'd had with this chap. Maybe the guy was mad and that's all there was to it. He'd check with Bill. He remembered a Stephenson: Jim, he thought. He'd arrested him for fraud many years ago. He'd been a nasty customer and had threatened all sorts. But this guy wasn't called Stephenson: he was sure of that. Maybe he had been using a false name. That was unlikely if he was dead. They probably would have got his real name for the death cert. Anyway if it was a false name it could be anybody; therefore he would have to assume it was his real name.

Now that he had opened the parcel and was totally confused as to its purpose he felt more panicky than before he opened it. He wished the hell that Bill hadn't called in or that the old guy hadn't died or that he wasn't such a wimp himself. He knew he should really go shopping for his tea but he hadn't the heart to go out so he settled for toast and marmalade. He would call into the station and see Bill in the morning and sort things out. He had his tea and then sat down and watched the news on the television. After a while he looked at the television properly and noticed that the news had finished. Thank God there was nobody asking questions about it. He hadn't heard a word. As he couldn't concentrate he switched off the television and wandered around the garden. He had an uneasy feeling in the pit of his stomach. He then went into the house and wandered around there. A couple of times he looked at the book and it seemed to spook him. It was like an evil charm lying there. He felt like throwing it in the bin or burning it. If Bill couldn't throw any light on it in the morning he would chuck it away. He decided to go the pub just to get out of its presence.

"Christ, I'm cracking up" he said to himself as he left the house. The pub was only a two minute walk away and he felt better when he went inside. It was noisy and warm and comforting. There were two of his friends there and they were in the middle of a conversation about the development of radar during the war, a subject he knew nothing about. He increasingly found he shared less and less common ground with his cronies. They would talk about foreign places they had taken a holiday in or a great book they had just read or a film they had seen that day. He could never muster up enough enthusiasm to do these things. On a night like this he would say to himself that he would go and see a film in the cinema the next day. Why not? What was there to stop him? His time was his own and money wasn't that tight and God knows he had no other arrangements or engagements to get in the way. He would plan to see a three o'clock show. That would give him time to get lunch, see the movie, shop for his tea on the way home and still be able to have his tea at six o'clock. The routine was sacred. The routine was all. But by the next morning everything would have changed. He would know in his heart as he lay in bed that he wasn't going to the cinema that day. All the enthusiasm garnered from his friends' conversation the previous evening had disappeared completely. He'd just make a list and go shopping. It felt safe. It felt .... safe.

That night he had his usual two pints and then said his goodbyes and went home. He felt that if he hadn't turned up that night, nobody would have missed him; nobody would have been worse off.

As he went into the house he saw the parcel again. He would bring it to the station in the morning and get it sorted out and get it out of his head.

CHAPTER 11

The early orders to join Peter's DVD club soon fell away. What were needed were regular advertising boosts but he couldn't afford these.

"You really need a big company behind you to get something like this off the ground properly" advised Charlie's advert guy.

'Now he tells me' thought Peter to himself. 'His specialist subject on Mastermind should be 'wise after the event". Maybe that should be Peter's also.

He struggled on and did his best to keep his head above water. He started copying the DVDs and selling pirate copies to try and make ends meet. He knew he would be in deep water if he was found out but he was running out of options. He'd give it six months and then make a decision to pull out or keep going. But if he pulled out he had nothing. Everything was hired or rented. He would be left with nothing and worse.

Six months turned to a year and he was getting deeper and

deeper into debt. The nice man who has lent him the money was nowhere to be seen. His business associates were not as pleasant as he had been at the beginning and indeed some seemed downright nasty. He was living on borrowed time, probably literally. He went north to visit Charlie to ask for help. He knew he would not get a favourable response, even with his life in danger. Charlie's principles were his principles and he was unlikely to change his mind. Charlie was delighted to see Peter. They had dinner. At least Peter had: Charlie only picked at his food. After dinner Peter was well relaxed by the wine and port. He broached the money problem. Charlie talked around the topic but the bottom line was he was not going to lend him money. Peter didn't protest because he had known the answer before he had headed north.

He was only back home three days when he had a telephone call from a nurse in the surgical ward of the Glasgow Royal Infirmary. She said that Mr. Osgood had asked her to phone and pass on the message that he had undergone emergency surgery for a bowel obstruction. Peter was shocked.

"Is he OK?" was all he could muster.

"Stable at the moment but we'll know more in a few days."

"I'll try and get up to see him. Tell him that, will you? But say I can't promise."

"He asked me to tell you he'll contact you when he's better."

"OK. Thank you nurse. Goodbye."

Peter stood for a long time at the phone with thought after thought speeding through his head. One line of thought was remembering Charlie's poor appetite when he had visited him just a few days ago. He hoped he was going to be alright. If he died he would feel very alone in the world.

The other train of thought was considering the consequences of Charlie dying. He tried to get this line of thinking out of his head, but it kept slipping back in. It made him feel guilty. He slept poorly that night and the next morning rang the hospital. He was eventually put through to the correct ward and spoke to a different nurse. He asked after Charlie's health.

"And who may I say is enquiring?"

"Peter Foster. I'm an old friend."

"Oh yes. Mr. Foster. You are down, of course, as his next of kin."

That was a surprise to Peter. He had never heard Charlie talk of family. He knew his wife was dead and he was childless. But to be put down as his next of kin: that was strange. The unwanted line of thought put its head above the parapet as Peter tried to listen to the nurse over the sound of his thoughts.

"So we think he's over the worst. I'll tell him you rang."

With that she hung up. He was going to pull through. That was excellent news, really excellent news. Wasn't it? He should pop up and see him. After all he was the next of kin, even though he wasn't kin at all. The bad thoughts were waving at him from afar. No, it was great news that he would get better, really great news.

He headed north once again the next day. By now he was glad to leave the city and probably would have gone to Antarctica by choice; however Glasgow would have to do. Charlie was in good form but certainly looked like he'd been through the mill.

"Why don't you come down and stay with me for convalescence. You can't look after yourself immediately at home."

"It's OK. I'll go to a nursing home. The hospital will recommend a good one. Sure you'd be no good at nursing the sick, no offence."

"None taken. I'd get you a nurse to look after you at my house. She could live in and look after you."

Charlie said nothing.

"That's decided then. I'll ask the nurse at the Infirmary when you'll be fit to travel south and I'll make all the arrangements. And just to warn you she will be more Hattie Jacques than Jessica Lange."

"Thanks a lot pal" Charlie said and smiled and then added "Seriously though, I'm grateful. And how is Petra or whatever her name is? Has she not moved in yet?"

"No. I told you we are taking it slowly. Anyway I'm not letting a dirty old man like you near her."

"The way I feel at the moment I wouldn't worry Peter. Cindy Crawford would be safe with me these days."

They said their goodbyes. Peter drove south (unusually for him) slowly not sure what to think.

CHAPTER 12

Greg woke up the next morning and was scared. He always thought that waking up with some purpose in his life again would be wonderful. He should jump out of bed, do 20 press-ups, have a cold shower and then do a two mile run. But he just felt scared. He would have to face his old comrades (some of them anyway). Maybe he'd like it but as he lay in bed he felt the whole thing would be tedious. Deep down he knew this was why he'd never visited them before. Hopefully Bill would sort out why he had been given this gardening notebook or diary or whatever it was. He had an uneasy feeling in the back of his mind that when he entered the station with the notebook under his arm there would be an outbreak of widespread laughter and they would come over to him, clap him on the back and say what a good sport he was. He knew in his head that they wouldn't do that to him, but his heart was slightly worried all the same.

As he was having breakfast he picked up the book again. He skipped onto March.

March 20: Got hanging baskets started in glasshouse. Worked well last year. Had a nice mature display early in season.

March 28: Cucumber seeds sown in propagator. Will need . . . . .

He flicked back to January again. He was staring at the page when he noticed something written in smaller writing at the bottom of the page.

He's still driving in here too fast in his fancy car.

He read it twice. It seemed out of place with the rest of the gardening information. He looked for more statements of a similar nature. At the foot of the Feb 3rd page he read.

He's got his wife, or whatever she is, a new car. One of those sporty jobs. Money to burn.

This was very odd. Slightly further on there was a gardening entry with a cryptic note underneath.

Feb 28th: She who was spoiled has flown the nest. Ha Ha!!

Greg skipped onto June.

June 5: Potatoes earthed up today. Strawberries have grey mould. Will need to treat.

He noticed at the bottom of the page a note in smaller writing.

Great day. SP has sold the fancy car and now has only a van.

What did that mean? Again it seemed out of keeping with the rest of the notebook. He moved on a few pages and saw another note at the bottom of the page away from the main notes.

SP doesn't look well. Clothes shabby. Unshaven.

SP. Who was that? He looked at the blank wall for inspiration. He turned to the next page.

SP has rough looking friends. Three heavies called to the house. What line of business is he in?

"Curiouser and curiouser" thought Greg feeling as surprised as Alice. At least he felt he had found some possible reason for him to have the book. There was more to it than gardening. What it was about was anybody's guess. He hadn't a clue. He turned to August.

August 12: Tops of tomato plants pinched out. Onions nearly ready.

More stuff taken from SP's house. He really must be in queer street.

Should he show this to Bill or would he try and work it out himself? He realized the tension and fear had evaporated. He had found something to occupy his mind. It was like meeting an old friend again. It felt comfortable and reassuring. He looked for more of the foot notes.

September 20: Turnips and carrots lifted. Packed in sand in back of big shed. Clearly labeled this year.

Brussels sprouts staked. Spring cabbages planted.

Summer shading washed off greenhouse. Some spring flower seeds sown.

Pots with Chrysanthemums, Azaleas and Cinerarias moved indoors.

SP arrived with older man. Interestingly older man nods at me in acknowledgement. SP has never made any effort to engage with me even though I see him driving in most evenings. Rude man.

September 21: Rest of tomatoes picked. Green ones put on window sills in small shed. Rest of day spent cleaning and disinfecting greenhouse.

SP must be doing a runner or more likely going on holidays. Old man must be house sitting.

September 22: Daffodils and crocuses planted. Lawns spiked and scarified. Started lifting potatoes.

Nurse arrived at SP's. Must be looking after old man. Still there when I left.

September 23: Lifted potatoes all day. Back breaking.

Nurse comes out of SP's house with her mobile phone ringing. God protect me from pretentious ring tones. It's that record Mr. C. has. John McCormack singing something or other.

September 25: Intended to pick and store all the apples. Didn't finish. Mayhem at SP's. Old man found dead. Police and ambulance attending. Police calling to the neighbours. I hear them ringing the door here. All drive away in the end.

September 28: Raspberry canes cut down. Greenhouse fumigated.

SP is back from hols or where ever he was. Police hot on his heels. Inside a long time. ???Trouble.

A mention of police brought the notes nearer to home.

Maybe there was something here. But what? He would need to consult Bill and get this gardener's address. It seemed that SP had lived beside or opposite him. If he knew the identity of SP then he might be able to work out the identity of the old man who died and what the police had found out about it.

He continued to leaf through the pages of the notebook to look for further relevant entries.

CHAPTER 13

"I've organized the nurse but there is a bit of bad news. Well maybe you won't think it is bad news. I have to go to the Pyrenees."

Peter was on the phone to Charlie in the hospital.

"Oh right. Is it that time of year already? No, it doesn't matter. I'll just get something organized up here."

"No it's all sorted. I've already hired a nurse who'll live in the week I'm away. I'd love to help you out in this way. I owe you so much"

"Well it's very kind. They're chucking me out on Tuesday so I'll be there Tuesday evening."

"No you won't. I'll be there Monday evening and I'll collect you Tuesday morning. It's all arranged. Don't you worry. Just relax and I'll take care of everything."

"OK. See you Tuesday morning then. If you change your mind, let me know; I'll understand. I wouldn't want to be stuck looking after me. I'm a prickly bastard when I'm hanging around. I like being busy."

"We'll be fine. The nurse will keep you in check. 'Bye."

Peter hung up the phone and stood looking at the wall. He had three days before picking up Charlie. It would drag. He'd try and keep busy and hopefully the time would slip away. He would try and put Charlie out of his mind. Anyway his business was slipping down the toilet. He really should concentrate on that. But he found it hard to concentrate. He was tired. He wasn't sleeping well. He was in dire financial straits. He had sold the big car and bought a van. What a come down. He was driving around in a white van. But he was doing a lot of the grafting himself and found the van handy. Gone were the days when he employed staff to do the dog work; now he was it. He'd sold his gold watch, given to him by Helen when they married. Despite everything, he found it hard to let it go. But needs must, so it went. The next thing to go would be the house. But he couldn't let that happen. He'd sort it out. He would. As well as the worry of being penniless and homeless he also had the threat of two broken legs or worse from the nice man who had lent him all that money. That's what kept him awake at night, sweating, heart racing and thinking; always thinking. His mind seemed to never shut down. He sometimes felt he was going mad. Possible solutions to his problems swirled around in his head. But he could never grasp one that would actually help or at least he tried not to think of grasping the one that would help. He felt that if he kept thinking something acceptable would present itself. What a change around in his life. One year ago he had everything; now he had nothing. It was all his own fault. Despite Helen screwing him for all he had he didn't feel bitter. He still loved her. How could he have been so stupid? The old story, he supposed.

He eventually poured himself a drink. And then another and then a third. He still couldn't relax. He knew he should ring Peta but he knew he couldn't concentrate to have a sensible conversation with her. She was asking more and more questions about what was bothering him. She said he looked drawn and pale and was losing weight. Peter felt she might be using this as an excuse to move in – needing the care of a good woman and all that. Peta wasn't exactly motherly but he felt she wanted to bring their relationship to a new level of commitment. Peter had half convinced himself, mainly by telling other people, that they both wanted to take things slowly. However he knew deep down that he was the one dragging his feet. Maybe when he got back from his trip and his finances were back in order and ....

"Christ, the sooner I get this sorted, the better" he thought to himself.

He poured himself another large measure of whiskey and headed off to bed hoping the alcohol might help him get some sleep.

CHAPTER 14

Greg got to the station at about 8.30 in the morning. He wanted to get to Bill before he went out. Sure enough Bill was in his office talking on the phone in a slightly restrained voice. When he hung up he looked up and saw Greg. His face lit up.

"I didn't think you'd come."

"Hey, come on; you know me better than that."

"Chief Constable's secretary, no sorry PA, hassling me for monthly figures" Bill said nodding towards the phone. "This isn't the job I signed up to 20-odd years ago. You're better off out of it. You really are. Come on and meet some of the old timers like ourselves."

"Before we do that I'd like to talk to you about the .... eh .... package you gave me; you know, from the dead bloke."

"Yeah. I remember."

"Where did he live?"

"Gosh .... eh .... I don't know off-hand. I could find out

from, eh …. let's see, Jackie was on the case. I'll give her a ring. Sit down for a sec."

As he dialed a number Bill looked at Greg and raised his eyebrows in a quizzical fashion.

"Just the address is it?"

"Yeah, thanks. Sorry for the bother."

As Bill was waiting for the phone to be answered he addressed Greg.

"I think he lived alone. The house is empty now. But I'm not sure. Why the interest though?"

"No, it's just …. well …. it's nothing really."

At that moment for some reason Greg had decided to keep the information in the notebook to himself. He didn't know why. It just seemed better that way.

Bill then started talking on the phone. It appeared to be Jackie. He was nodding and making appropriate noises down the line. He finished the call with a few "yeahs" and "thank yous".

"Jackie says he lived at 3 Foundling Lane, out off the Empton Road. You know the place."

Greg nodded. He would go out there and see what was what. He spent the rest of the morning chatting with old comrades and supping tea in the canteen. He enjoyed the adulation he received, even from those who had joined after he had retired. He did seem to have a good reputation and was a bit of a local legend. It did cheer him up immensely; it was like his batteries had been recharged. He had lunch there and afterwards said his goodbyes. He was asked to make sure he came back soon and he assured them he would. As he walked out of the station to his car he felt he would love to return soon but he knew in a day or two he would lose that feeling which would be replaced by a fear of going there again. Why he would be afraid he didn't know but it seemed to be part of getting old. It was for him anyway.

He had a vague idea where Foundling Lane was and drove in that general direction. After a few wrong turns he found the place. It was in a row of six cottages. The front doors were on the street with no front gardens. Opposite the cottages was an open field. The garden must be around the back. Greg walked to the end of the block and went around the back. The cottages had very small gardens and the back of number 3 seemed to only have a yard with no actual garden. He was puzzled. This scene didn't fit in with the information in the notebook. Was all this gardening stuff just a fantasy? It certainly didn't go on here at number 3. He went around to the front again and looked around. He couldn't picture where SP lived if the gardener (if that what he was) saw him coming and going. He'd have to clarify matters with Bill. He could ask one of the neighbours but he felt that it would not be appropriate. The guy was dead and he felt that he himself had no official capacity or business. Jackie must have thought he was talking about another case. It could be sorted out. He didn't want to appear too anxious about the matter in case Bill demanded to know more. He was still unsure of his motives for the secrecy but at the back of his mind he thought there might be something important to be discovered and, to be honest, he didn't want to share any glory with anyone else. It was strange. When he was on active duty he was never the one to seek glory or praise. He tried to keep his head below the parapet and avoid any publicity. It didn't sit well on his shoulders. Now he seemed to be hoping for the praise and glory. Maybe it was the respect he had got at the station that morning. He knew it was gained from his work in the past. What he had done since retiring would not earn him the respect of an ant. He felt the morning's adulation was now undeserved. Maybe he wanted to earn that respect again, now, today. He'd leave it a day and ring Bill the day after tomorrow. He would go back and examine the notebook further.

CHAPTER 15

Peter sat on the plane back from Perpignan. He had a lovely week spoiled at the end by the news from the police that Charlie was dead. They told him he had been hit on the head. There had been no sign of a break-in. He'd have to come straight home. They had telephoned his hotel in Banyuls-sur-mer where he was booked to stay the night he finished his trek. He had spent the last five years doing the GR10 trek across the Pyrenees from Hendaye on the Atlantic side to Banyuls-sur-mer on the Mediterranean side. To do it in as a single journey would take a few weeks. He never had that sort of time. Therefore he had done the trek in five separate parts. He was feeling good about completing it as he arrived at the Thalacap Catalogne to have a meal and go to bed for a well earned rest. As he checked in he sensed something was wrong. The manager of the hotel had checked his name and address and passport three times. When he was sure he had the correct man he gave the message that the police in Britain wanted him to call them on an urgent matter. He called them as requested and got the news about Charlie. Now as he sat on the plane he wondered how the police would handle him. He said he would go straight to the station when he returned but the police said they would prefer to call to the house. All the forensic examinations of the property had been completed and so interviewing him in the house would suit them better. He didn't mind. The house would probably be in a mess but what the hell. Surprisingly he slept intermittently on the flight. That was the anti-travel sickness pill kicking in rather than him being relaxed about arriving home to this situation. He had never been a friend of the police. He had never been in trouble with them directly but had kept his distance. He felt uncomfortable in their presence. Some of his business dealing in the past had been slightly dodgy, but no more than the next bloke's. He wasn't ashamed or guilty; but he would have preferred to avoid the police.

He had left his car at the airport. He paid for his parking and then drove home. He was normally a speed merchant but today he kept under the speed limit. He wasn't sure whether this was to delay his meeting with the police or whether it reflected a desire not to be charged with speeding just before meeting the police who were investigating a more serious crime. He found driving at the speed limit quite relaxing, if slow. He wondered what they'd ask him. He hoped they wouldn't stay too long. He wanted a shower and a sit down. He wanted to meet Peta. He didn't want a long and stressful questioning session with the police. It couldn't be avoided so he might as well grin and bear it. He drove up to the front door. He left his luggage and went in. The house was surprisingly tidy and there was little, if any, sign of it being a crime scene. He telephoned the police immediately, although he was tempted to shower first. He then got the luggage from the car and left it in the hall. He was going to pour himself a drink but then thought the better of it. He thought that might tarnish his image with the police; what image? He paced up and down the living room. They were taking their time. God damn them, why couldn't they hurry up? He was getting twitchier by the minute.

At last he saw the police car coming up the drive. He wasn't sure whether he should open the door without them ringing the doorbell or wait for them to ring it. He didn't want to appear too anxious so he decided to keep cool and wait for them to ring the doorbell. When they did so he stood up straight, shook his head and cleared his throat. He then walked to the front door and opened it.

"Come in gentlemen please. Come in."

CHAPTER 16

Back at home Greg got a notebook out and decided to write all the footnotes in the form of a continuous narrative. When he had finished he reviewed the outcome.

He's still driving in here too fast in his fancy car.

He's got his wife, or whatever she is, a new car. One of those sporty jobs. Money to burn.

She who was spoiled has flown the nest. Ha Ha!!

Great day. SP has sold the fancy car and now has only a van.

SP doesn't look well. Clothes shabby. Unshaven.

Big lorry came and took away a lot of furniture and all his gym equipment. Interesting??

SP's garden getting out of hand. Must have sacked that so-called gardener. I wouldn't have let him cut the grass.

SP arrived with older man. Interestingly older man nods at me in acknowledgement. SP has never made any effort to engage with me even though I see him driving in most evenings. Rude man.

SP must be doing a runner or more likely going on holidays. Old man must be house sitting.

Nurse arrived at SP's. Must be looking after old man. Still there when I left.

Nurse comes out of SP's house with her mobile phone ringing. God protect me from pretentious ring tones. It's that record Mr. C. has. John McCormack singing something or other.

Mayhem at SP's. Old man found dead. Police and ambulance attending. Police calling to the neighbours. I hear them ringing the door here. All drive away in the end.

SP is back from hols or where ever he was. Police hot on his heels. Inside a long time. ???Trouble.

Police in and out again.

Police back again. SP must have been a naughty boy. HaHa!

Things look better for SP. Got a nice car again. Whistling a lot. Very annoying.

Tripped and fell getting out of the car. Normally I would go and help. Not with SP though.

Snooker table being moved into SP's house. Things definitely looking up for him. Still a snooty bugger.

The gym stuff came back today

I don't believe it. A van with Sotheby's written on the side delivered two paintings to him. What a poser.

SP continues to look cocky. I'd love to take him down a peg or two.

Another new car. Bentley I think. What next. He certainly doesn't hide his wealth.

All of the above entries had been under some gardening information. What did it all mean? For some reason it excited Greg. Was there something to all this or was it the ravings of a demented old man? After all he didn't seem to have a garden despite all the stuff in the notebook.

He went out to the shops and got himself a ready-made lasagna and garlic bread for his tea. He had always liked Italian food and at one time had thought of retiring to Italy. Like everything else these days, he never did anything about it. He had mentioned it in the pub one night and everybody had said it was a great idea.

"Sure you've no ties or anything. Why not do it? Eh, why not?"

He couldn't think of a good reason for not going: apart from inertia and fear. Fear of what? He didn't know. It was more of this free-floating fear that seemed to dominate his life these days. It stopped him from doing simple things like going to the cinema and bigger things like going away on holidays. Moving to Italy? Who was he fooling? After tea he watched the television news. He was planning to go to the pub but he decided on an early night instead. He went to bed and started turning over things in his mind in the hope of making some sense of the notebook the dead guy had sent to him. It seemed he was probably going to bring it to the police station instead of posting it as only his name and the police station were written on the package, which was by no means a full address. It was written in pencil which was another factor against it being posted. He probably would have explained things to Greg and made it all clear. Of course there was the distinct possibility he was a loony. God knows he had met plenty of them in the course of his work over the years. He fervently hoped he wasn't one of them. He wanted this to amount to something so as *he* could amount to something again. Keeping all the details to himself was awkward but he felt that if he told Bill, Bill would share any glory (or as a serving officer take it all). Greg also thought if the guy was mad he didn't want to be made to look a fool by taking it seriously. Maybe the whole thing was crazy. At one level he was upset, maybe even angry (although he hadn't felt an emotion that strong or passionate in a long time), that this package had upset his cosy routine. At another level he was thankful of the distraction. He was still swithering between these two emotions. Anyway he'd ring Bill in the morning and sort out the guy's address. Hopefully he'd been given the wrong one.

CHAPTER 17

Peter offered the two detectives a cup of tea but they politely refused. They went through the usual preliminaries. They told him that Mr. Osgood was found dead in Peter's house four days ago. He had been killed by multiple blows from a blunt instrument to the head. They needed him to fill in a lot of details about the circumstances of Mr. Osgood being at Peter's house.

"Well, Charlie, Mr. Osgood, and I go back a long way. He supported me in my early business ventures and always gave me solid advice. He had taken ill up in Scotland where he had gone when he retired."

"Pardon me Mr. Foster what line of business was Mr. Osgood in?"

"He imported and exported things. I'm not quite sure exactly what. He advised *me* in business rather than the reverse."

"We've not been able to find out much about his business

interests either. Anyway, proceed. I'm sorry to have interrupted you."

"Well, he has no family that I know of so I made an offer to him to come and stay with me when he was discharged from the hospital. Then I realized I was going to finish my trek across the Pyrenees at that time and rang him back. However he was set on coming down and said he would organize a nurse while I was on vacation and we could catch up when I returned."

"Yes the nurse interests us a lot. What do you know about her?"

"Nothing really. She was to arrive the day after I left so I never met her and Charlie never said anything about her. Sorry."

"We thought that's what you'd say. Anyway go on."

"Well I did my five day trek across the Pyrenees and when I got to the hotel at the end of my journey I got the message you wanted to get in touch. And here we are."

"Did a group of you go on this trek?"

"No just me by myself. I have done the rest of it in small stages over the last four years, but always alone. It is very enjoyable. Being out of contact with the world is very stress-free and relaxing. I would recommend it to anyone. I remember reading about the Polar explorers at the end of the nineteenth century and the beginning of the twentieth century. I was jealous of their complete isolation from the world. Shackelton and his party didn't even know how the 14-18 war was progressing. I think it is the best kind of holiday you can have."

"Yes, very interesting Mr. Foster but did you know you are the sole beneficiary of Mr. Osgood's will? He doesn't appear to have any other family."

"No, I didn't know that. We never spoke of such matters. Charlie was a man of the world in one way but liked his privacy and guarded it very carefully. That's why I never knew any of his business details and why you are finding it hard to get any such details. Some people used to insinuate that such privacy stank of illegality. But I don't think so. Charlie liked to keep these things to himself. They were nobody else's business."

"Is there anything else you want to tell us?" the smaller of the two detectives asked with what was the first menacing tone in the interview.

"Eh."

Peter thought hard and after a suitable pause said

"No. I can't think of anything else really. If I do where can I contact you gentlemen?"

The smaller man gave him a card and pointed to the phone number at the top.

"If I'm not there, ask for DS Collins. That's 'im" he said pointing at the taller of the two men.

Peter looked carefully at the card and then put it in his top pocket.

"If there's nothing else we'll be on our way. Not planning any more trips abroad in the near future Mr. Foster, are you?"

"No, that's me until next year probably" Peter replied laughing, trying to make light of the implied threat in the detective's question.

They shook hands and the two detectives left Peter in the house looking very pensive.

CHAPTER 18

He woke up the next morning and felt refreshed. He was anxious to get up and get going. This was a foreign feeling to him. Sometimes as he lay in bed in the morning he would convince himself that he really wanted to get up and face the day. However he knew deep down that this was just an act to try and cheer himself up. It was pathetic really. But today was different: he really did feel energized. He got up and went downstairs in his dressing gown to phone Bill. It was 8.30. He should be in by now. He dialed the number and spoke to the girl on the switchboard. He didn't recognize her voice and she didn't make any sign of knowing him. He was told that Bill's extension was engaged but would he like to hold on. He said he would. He waited for about five minutes although it felt like five hours. Eventually the girl said she was putting him through and he heard Bill's voice sounding rather tetchy.

"Bill it's Greg. Sorry to bother you so early. I just need to ask you a quick question if you have a minute."

Bill's voice mellowed.

Hi Greg. Doin'OK? Yeah, fire ahead."

"I don't want to labour the point but I need to check that old guy's address, you know the one who left the package for me in his house the day he died. The address you got from Jackie was wrong. At least I think it was."

"I don't know much about it but I can check with Jackie and get back to you later. Is that OK?"

"Sure. Again, sorry for the bother. You're a pal."

"Speak to you later Greg. Take it easy."

Greg hung the phone up and resigned himself to the wait. He should have done the shopping first. Now he was afraid to leave the house to go shopping in case he missed Bill's call. He made some tea and toast and sat beside the phone, staring at it and willing it to ring. He went upstairs but didn't have a shower in case he missed the phone. He got dressed and wandered aimlessly around the house. Bill was a busy man. He would probably forget to ask Jackie about the address. She might be out all day. It was pointless hanging around. He should have got that answer phone thing the BT man offered him. He didn't like being phoned at home and offered a free this and a free that. He always knew there was a catch. When the BT man offered him this answer phone service he asked about getting a machine to record the messages. He had been told there was no machine. He would just call a number and his messages would be played back. That couldn't be secure; couldn't be private. Anyway it was a rip off. He didn't need an answer phone and they were trying to sell him something he didn't want. Well not exactly sell it, as he was told there was no charge. But they would charge him some way or other. No free lunches and all that. Still he now wished he could leave the house knowing that Bill could get a message to him if he rang back. Anyway he was going to the shops and he could ring Bill tomorrow if he missed the call today when he was out.

The shopping was a briefer affair than usual. He was back within the hour. He looked at the phone to see if he could ascertain (?how) if it had rung or not. He'd probably missed the call and had resigned himself to that fact. He'd ring tomorrow and sort it out. He pretended he'd forgotten all about the call as he busied himself doing little jobs around the house. But he had one ear cocked in hopeful anticipation, a hope that was unfulfilled that day. By 11pm he had consciously and unconsciously and in every way possible given up the idea that Bill would call back that night. He fell asleep and slept more soundly than he thought he would.

He awoke the next day and his first thought was to ring Bill. Then he wondered if Bill would feel he was being pestered, particularly if Bill hadn't phoned back the previous day. He decided to put off ringing until lunchtime. Again there was the dilemma of staying in or going out and risking missing the phone. He stayed in and no call came. At 1.00 he reckoned that Bill would be having a sandwich in his office and decided to make the call. He was told that Bill was away on a training day. Disappointingly he was about to thank the operator and hang up when he suddenly asked to speak to Jackie Forbes. It seemed an automatic reaction. The thought hadn't reached his conscious mind when he heard himself asking to speak to her. After a minute he heard a woman's voice at the other end of the phone.

"D.S. Forbes here. How can I help you?"

"Jackie, it's Greg O'Connor. You know, I was in the other day with Bill."

"Ah Greg, how are you? Are you looking for Bill?"

"Well no. It's you I'm looking for actually. Have you got a minute?"

He had never known Jackie well. She had joined the station after he had retired and he just knew her from meeting up at official functions he had attended before his retirement. He carried on cautiously.

"You probably won't remember but Bill rang you a few days ago to ask the address of the old man who was found dead at home. He had had a package addressed to me in his house. Bill dropped it out to my house a few days ago. I was just...."

"Yeah, I remember. It was ...eh... that bloke .....eh.... he lived out, you know, off the Empton Road: Foundling Lane, I think. Yes, it was Foundling Lane."

"Are you sure that's the right address?"

"I'm pretty sure but let me check. Can you hold a sec?"

Greg was glad she had not said she would ring him back. That would have been more waiting and missed shopping. Maybe for the moment he should go back to a once daily shopping trip until all this carry-on was over. Or maybe even a weekly shop. No, wait, no need to over react. He was startled out of his thoughts by the sound of Jackie's voice.

"Yeah, that's the right address. 3 Foundling Lane. That's definitely his home address. It's where his body was found."

"And your parcel" she added as an afterthought.

He decided to show some of his hand to Jackie.

"Do you know if he was a keen gardener? It may sound like a strange question but ...."

"Well I don't know how keen he was, but it was what he did for a living. He had been a professional gardener for someone up on Oak Heights. It was one of those big houses they built there a few years ago."

Now it became clear to Greg. The notebook was a professional record of the garden he looked after for his employer. That's why he had found no garden at his home address.

"Thanks Jackie. That's great. If Bill asks you about it just tell him we've been in direct contact and things are sorted. Thanks again."

"Glad to be of service sir" she replied in mock Jeeves-type voice.

Greg felt progress had been made. The one thing that pleased him most was that the old guy was not raving. He had made genuine gardening notes. Therefore the SP thing (whatever it was) must also be kosher. Oak Heights - now that was interesting. He now thought he knew who SP was. That was very interesting.

CHAPTER 19

He needed the file on the Charlie Osgood murder. He should have recognized the references to that crime sooner. It was all the gardening stuff had confused him. And he was a confused old man to start with anyway and he would need the file to refresh his memory of the crime. The old gardener must have given Peter Foster the initials SP. Greg couldn't work out why unless he knew Foster previously living under an alias. That wouldn't have surprised Greg. There was nothing he had found in the notebook that seemed particularly relevant to providing new information in the case. Obviously the background given by the gardener's observations would be interesting and even helpful in building up a profile of Foster. But that had all been done and it had not got them much further. Anyway he'd get the file and take things from there.

He foresaw two problems with getting the case file. Firstly he may not be given it. He was retired and strictly speaking he had no business accessing confidential case files. However he was sure he could twist Bill's arm to look the other way. He would only need it for 24 hours. The second problem was what to tell Bill. If he explained the situation Bill would want to take over and claim all the credit. Well, he might. But if he didn't explain things then Bill may not want to hand over the file. What to do? Yes, that might do it. He'd tell him he had been thinking over the case at home and something had been niggling at him and he just couldn't nail the thought. He'd say that he thought he could put his mind at rest if he could have the file for 24 hours. That should be enough to convince Bill. Now should he telephone or call in? He'd not been in touch for ages and now he was almost harassing the man. It couldn't be helped. He'd phone first and that would give Bill a chance to request and get the file for Greg to collect.

His mind wandered back on the case and he felt "at home" with these professional thoughts rather than deciding whether he should have lasagna or Bolognese for his tea. He felt like a bald man whose hair had grown back while he was asleep. He was content and happy. Maybe he should have taken up some of the consulting and security jobs he was offered around the time of his retirement. At the time he thought a clean break was best. He had felt reasonably secure financially and so, he had asked himself, why work? But more recently he worried about money and getting looked after as he got older and probably more frail. It would be good to have some sort of income over and above his paltry pension. And now that he was working on a case again and feeling so positive and energized he felt he had made a mistake in his complete retirement. But now all he hoped was that this would all lead to something. It felt it would be a real feather in his cap if he could do something to bring the Osgood case to a conclusion. Maybe it was unfinished business for him. He had never thought of it as such before but it would be a hell of a thing to sort it out now, even though he was retired. All the new recruits that didn't know him but had heard of him probably thought he was yesterday's news. Reputations disappear quickly. But to come up trumps on this: that would be today's headlines. He sat in his chair lost in thought about the past and his great triumphs. He had had legendary status: everybody told him so. He believed them. Well the legend was coming back.

He went to bed that night happier than he'd felt in years. He'd have the case file in the next few days and hopefully he'd have a clearer idea of things then. Roll on tomorrow.

CHAPTER 20

The police came to see Peter Foster many times in the next few months. He had gone down to the station to make a formal statement. After this the visits comprised of going over the same ground again and again. They were clearly at a loss as to who murdered Charlie. He wished he could give more help but he had told them all he could. There were questions about his financial status. He had admitted things were tight but he told them that was par for the course in the business world today. He knew they thought that he had killed Charlie or at least had arranged for Charlie to be killed. His motive was huge: £3.8 million. That was the final total of Charlie's estate. It was certainly a good motive for murder. They kept at him like a dog with a bone but they got nowhere. There was nowhere to go. He had an iron-clad alibi. The old guy, O'Connor, was tenacious. He would love to have framed him for the crime. But he couldn't pin anything on him. He thought of moving to Spain but he

stayed around just for the hell of it. He was never smart or
angry or stubborn or awkward with the police. In fact he was
always a perfect gentleman even when they were not. He co-
operated fully in their enquiries and the police had no cause
to complain about him. That is what made the O'Connor guy
really mad. Eventually the visits tailed off and the case more
or less dropped off everybody's radar. Peter got the money
from Charlie's estate and even with a hefty inheritance tax
he was able to pay off his loans (high interest included) and
everybody seemed happy - except the police, especially Greg
O'Connor. But then Peter heard that O'Connor had retired
and the whole investigation died a death completely. Peter
was able to invest in his new business and with saturation
advertising it took off. He was employing a staff of 30 based
on three different sites and he had a manager overseeing the
whole venture. He relaxed and lived the good life. Peta had
moved in and they seemed made for each other. He had the
best Italian wine, could listen to classical music all day if
he pleased and pop off for a holiday anywhere in the world
whenever he wished. He was enjoying the fruits of his labours. He knew that Charlie had been successful in business
but he had never seemed to enjoy life. There was always a
melancholy air around Charlie. His wealth was wasted on
him. But not on Peter – he knew how to party.

It was Peta's 40th birthday that day and they were having
a big bash to celebrate it. It was a no-expenses-spared affair.
Caviar flown in from the Black Sea, ice sculptures, proper
waitresses in black dresses and white aprons and the pièce de
résistance – Jools Holland providing the live music. Peter had
arranged it all. It was his way of showing his love and appre-
ciation. Peta was thrilled. The both appreciated such osten-

tatious celebrations. At the height of the party there were 70 people in the house and gardens. It was a great success. Peta was more than appreciative later that night. As he drifted off to sleep that night Peter thought that life was good.

CHAPTER 21

"Bill, it's me again. Sorry to keep bothering you."

"Not at all. Jackie told me you had sorted things out between you; that's right isn't it?"

"Oh yeah, that's fine thanks. It's just, well, you remember the Charlie Osgood case. I still feel that's unfinished business. I have being thinking about it over the last few weeks and, well, there are a few details I'd like to check in the case file. Is there any chance I could get a look at it?"

"You know the position Greg. Mmm let's see. I suppose you could access it in my office. But don't tell anybody. Just tell them you are checking your years of service because you have a gripe with pensions or something. I can't let you take it out of the station and I don't want people to know you're accessing the records. It might upset the brass if they got wind of it. You know what I mean."

"That would be wonderful. That's suit me fine. When will I come in?"

"I'll put in a requisition for the file today. It should be here in the morning. Come in about 11 o'clock tomorrow morning. If it doesn't arrive I'll ring you and we can reschedule your visit."

"11 o'clock in the morning. That's perfect. I really appreciate this Bill, thanks. See you in the morning."

"Yeah, bye."

Bill didn't seem to connect the package and the old gardener with Greg asking for the file.

'Some detective' thought Greg.

Anyway it was fine with him. If Greg could turn up something he would have to share the glory with no one.

He could see the newspaper headlines 'Retired Cop Solves Murder Case'. Of course the fact that the case was his to solve when he was still active on the force could conveniently be avoided for the present. Let him have his moment in the sun. Reality would probably kick in soon enough.

He decided he would take a run up to what had been the murder scene of Charlie Osgood all those years ago. He knew the way but it felt strange to him to feel he was on a "case" when he had been retired for so long. Still all the old instincts and reactions were back. Hell, it was good. He drove past the houses and parked. He sat for a while. All seemed quiet. He then got out of the car and walked slowly towards the group of houses where Peter Foster lived and Frederick Sims had worked. The house where Foster had lived (and maybe still lived) had two cars outside it: both looked expensive. He could see through to the back garden and there was a large gazebo and marquee erected there. With that a white van drove past Greg and up to the front door of the house. "Excelsior Catering" was written in red letters on the side. The driver rang the doorbell. Greg stepped behind a tree to get a look at what was happening without being seen himself. A tall lady in her thirties opened the door and spoke to the van driver. She then turned away and said something into the house. A moment later a man came to the door. He was all smiles. So was Greg because the man was Foster. A bit older now but it was definitely him. He hadn't moved away.

'My God, how interesting' he thought.

The catering van was unloaded and after a brief conversation with the woman it was driven off. Foster was nowhere to be seen. Greg wondered what was going on. He half thought of calling in and facing up to Foster again. But that could wait until he had accessed the file again and maybe gained some more insight into the case from the gardener's notes. There was no rush. He had waited all those years he could wait a few days longer. He fantasized that he would get concrete evidence against Foster and he would go and arrest him (technically that might be tricky as he had retired and Foster would know that) and see the look of fear on his face as he charged him with murder. Oh, that would be good. He could certainly die happy then. The sound of a car starting up jolted him back to reality. It was the woman leaving the house. Greg shuffled behind a tree where he thought he could not be seen from the road. As she drove past he got a chance to run his eyes quickly over her. She was a looker, for sure. Foster could pick 'em all right.

CHAPTER 22

Greg was up and at it early the next morning. He decided he would go shopping for his dinner before he went to the station. That way he could stay late if necessary and still have a nice dinner when he got home. He envisaged having lunch in the station canteen. He would have liked to discuss the case over lunch but Bill would kill him if he talked to anyone else about the case and he didn't want to go into details with Bill. So he would keep his own counsel.

He got there about 11.10. He didn't want to appear too anxious. He was let through to Bill's office. The office was empty but there was a note on the desk on top of an envelope. It read

Greg

Your time sheets are enclosed. Hope it helps to sort out your problem. Feel free to use my office for the day.

Look after the enclosed documents carefully.

Bill

Greg got the drift. He went back and closed the door. He sat at Bill's desk and opened the envelope. He took out a brown cardboard folder with all the bits and bobs associated with the Osgood murder. As usual they were in a mess. Was there someone employed to go around at night and muddle up these case files? Even the smallest and thinnest files were never in any sequence or order. He tried to sort out the various papers and reports into some sort of order. It took about an hour but it was important preliminary work.

Once things were sorted he began to check through witness statements to see if Frederick Sims had been interviewed. He didn't remember the name but nowadays that didn't mean much. He looked through the statements and Sims did not appear to have been interviewed. That reflected badly on the investigation but the good news was that Sims' notes on his observation of Foster may cast some new light on the subject. Up until now Greg couldn't see what form that enlightenment might take but hopefully by matching the case file and Sims' notes he would come up with something.

He looked at the first statement, that of George Crawford. He tried to remember Crawford. Yes, he looked a bit like Charlton Heston and had the biggest house in the development. He had a large greenhouse and …. Greg wondered if Sims had worked for Crawford. He would need to check that out. Anyway back to Crawford's statement.

I am George Crawford and I reside at The Grange House, Oak Heights, Shiperley.

I first became suspicious when the postman couldn't get an answer at the door of number 5 - Mains Court I think they call it. I knew the old man was staying there to recuperate from some surgery. Foster had mentioned it to me before he left for Spain, I think it was. I had also seen a nurse go in and out. I thought she might have been staying there as well because her car was there when I got up at 7.30 that morning. I had noticed that the postman had rung the door bell at about 9.30 in the morning and got no answer. I thought that the old man might not be up. I forgot about the nurse. When he came back about 3pm he still didn't get an answer. At that stage he came over to my house and rang the bell. He asked me if I would sign for a registered letter as he couldn't get an answer at the house. I hesitated because Foster could be an awkward individual and I didn't want him to think I would mess with his post. I stressed to the postman that somebody should be home but that he might be resting as he was recovering from surgery. The postman seemed taken aback when I said this but then I realized he thought I was talking about Foster himself. I explained things briefly to him. I asked him to walk back to the house with me. I rang the doorbell and we waited. There was no sound from the house. I informed the postman that I was going to look around the back of the house. He said he needed to be on his way but I asked him to wait in case someone answered the door. I noticed that the nurse's car was not there and then thought that she might have brought the old man out. However I was now half way round to the back of the house and so I continued. At that stage I remember hoping he had not gone out with the nurse. That seems a cruel thought now but at the time I did not want to look a fool. I came to the French windows at the back of the house leading from the house onto the patio on which I was then standing. I looked in through the window with a hand cupped over my right eye to block the light and get a clearer view. I thought I saw a body lying on the floor but wondered whether my eyes were playing tricks on me. I squinted and cupped my left hand over my left eye and looked again. Now I was fairly certain. I called the postman around and asked him to look in the window and tell me if he saw anything. He peered through the window for a moment and then pulled away suddenly taking a sharp intake of breath. His actions confirmed my suspicions. We decided to call the police. He had a mobile phone so we used that. I noted the time to be 3.20pm.

I had seen the nurse go into the house but I never spoke to her or had any contact with her. I am not sure when she came but I think she was there, or at least the car was there, the morning of the day I found the body. But I can't be sure of that. I never spoke to the old man either. He was sick or had been. That's why I thought he had collapsed and died of natural causes when I first saw the body.

I had not seen Mr. Foster for a week or so. As I said he told me he was going away for a couple of weeks.

Signed: *George Crawford*
Date: *20/8/00*

Greg sat and mulled over the contents of Crawford's statement. It was much as he remembered it. It didn't really clarify his thoughts about the case. He pressed on.

CHAPTER 23

Peter Foster woke up the next morning early: too early. He reflected in the success of last night's party. It was the way he had always pictured things should be for him. This was the life he was meant for. This was his fate and his destiny. It had taken more than he bargained for to get this far. Years ago if he had foreseen what he'd have to do to get to this luxurious life, would he have went ahead anyway? Would he have done all the things he had done? He couldn't, no, wouldn't answer that question. Not to anyone; not even to himself. Peta stirred and opened her eyes slowly.

"Thank you again for last night. It was wonderful."

Peter smiled and gave her a kiss on the head. He was undecided about getting up but in the end he made the break. He wandered down the stairs and put on some coffee. The place was clean and tidy which was another advantage of having money. The caterers were paid extra to clean the place up afterwards. It was great coming down to this order rather than the chaos and mess usually associated with the morning-after. He couldn't stand having to clean up: it would spoil the whole enjoyment of the previous evening. And he couldn't tolerate that. He knew he had become soft. There was a time he'd have endured any discomfort or suffering to get on in life. He had worked his way up from the bottom and he was content in himself that he had earned his privileges. OK, things had changed after his divorce and the events after that were unplanned. But he felt that these unplanned episodes did not detract from his overall sense of feeling that he deserved what he had achieved. He wasn't proud of everything he had done but then who was? At least he had made something of himself. His father had always told him that he was good for nothing and would never amount to anything. As a child he had felt worthless and that was just the way things were. But looking back now he knew it was madness. He never got praise from his father. In fact his father went out of his way to put him down at every opportunity. His mother got the same treatment. Neighbours and friends (well, people they knew at any rate) were unaware of the psychological battering that this man subjected his wife and son to. He was regarded as a loveable rogue; usually the worst for drink but pleasant with it. The never saw the other side of him. As a result Peter felt it was his own fault that his father never loved him. Not that he associated the word 'love' with his father. He just wanted some nod or wink of encouragement. He was sure his mother felt as guilty as he did but they never discussed it. All the money went on drink and because he was mostly drunk he could never hold down a job. As a result they were always poor. His father seemed proud of his poverty. It was a reverse type of snobbery. As a child Peter remembered thinking that not having money was better than having money. Under his father's influence his thinking about most things in life became warped. But the older he got he knew his father's views on life were crazy and wrong. Peter appreciated that he had the moral strength to pull himself out of the hole his father had put him in. His mother wasn't so lucky. She became agoraphobic and died a mental wreck within a few months of her husband drinking himself to death. Peter found his father's death liberating but his mother could not cope. She had developed a bizarre dependence on him despite the fact that her husband had made her life a misery. She couldn't survive without him. They had had a perverse symbiotic relationship. A buzz from the coffee machine brought him back to the present. He smiled to himself. Anyway he was content and happy now. He had a lovely house and partner and all the luxuries he wished for. Yes, life was good: it was better than ever.

CHAPTER 24

Greg continued to flick through the file. He looked at the other statements. There were statements from the postman, Mike McNeish and from another neighbour. They both basically agreed with George Crawford's statement. He then came to Peter Foster's statement. He thought he should remember it well as he had taken it himself. He glanced through it quickly. Yeah, it was just as he recalled. Foster's story was that Osgood was convalescing after an operation. He had invited him down to his house to recuperate. After he had made this arrangement he realized that at the same time he would be away completing a walk across the Pyrenees from the Atlantic side to the Mediterranean side. He had forgotten he was going on the walk when he invited Osgood to stay. However Osgood didn't appear to mind that Foster would be away for the beginning of his visit and told Foster that he would arrange a nurse to look after him. Foster said he went away as planned in the knowledge that the nurse would be arriving the next day. He went on the walk, one of the advantages of it being that you were out of contact with civilization during that time. When he got to the hotel at the Mediterranean end of the walk he got the message to telephone the police at home. It was then he found out about Osgood's murder and came straight back.

Greg thought it through again as he had done many times before. It was all so neat and tidy. They had searched for the nurse without any success. She had not been seen since the evening before the body had been found in the house. All local agencies were contacted first. The search was then extended to Scotland and when that drew a blank it was thrown open nationwide. Her car, described as a small black hatchback or small dark coloured car, was never traced. Some tyre tracks were found on the edge of the front lawn but were just another dead end. Osgood's home was searched and his bank records scrutinized but no trace of any arrangement between him and a nurse or nursing agency was found. Foster's garden and house were carefully searched to see if the nurse had been killed and her body hidden on the property. The considered the possibility she had been kidnapped but that never came to anything either. The working theories were that the nurse, either acting alone or with an accomplice, had murdered Osgood or that a person or persons unknown had murdered Osgood and the nurse and had hidden her body somewhere else. As the nurse was a completely unknown quantity no motive could be formulated to link her with the murder. Foster's accounts were carefully scrutinized and no payments could be traced to an unknown person. Indeed no payments of any magnitude had been made at all as Foster was obviously in dire financial straits. Greg was sure he borrowed money off some loan sharks but was unable to prove this. Osgood had left him everything in his will which came to 3.8 million pounds. After tax Foster would still have over 2 million. That was a motive for murder if ever there was one but he could not tie Foster into anything.

When he thought about it logically he supposed that he hoped to find some clue in the gardener's observations of Foster that might help to nail him. But what clue could that be? The observations of the gardener had certainly charted Foster's decline into poverty and his subsequent change of fortune. But Greg already knew about that and it did not help to nail Foster. He'd been through the various observations a few times and nothing seemed to help. Then he wondered if there were other volumes of the notebook written up for different years. He checked the cover of the one he had. It said "Gardener's Notes 2000". Was there a 1999 or 2001 version? They might provide further clues. He felt the excitement build up again. He would need to find out who was looking after the dead chap's estate and see if his house had been sold. He wasn't sure how to go about this as he had no official help and therefore nobody to do his donkey work. He decided to call out to the house and see if anyone was in. As he drove out he felt some apprehension as he had no official status. Should he pass himself off as a serving policeman or should he just make a general enquiry as to the possible whereabouts of the old man's belongings. He pulled up outside the house. There was no sign of activity but he noticed a "For Sale" sign up with the name of an estate agent in town. It was that one with the annoying advertisement on the radio where these women said they were moving in with this bloke who owned the estate agency. Moving in with him – nudge, nudge, wink, wink; but no, he's only acting as their agent. Oh, how hilarious. He went up and rang the bell but the only response was silence. Well at least he had the estate agent's name. That would be his next port of call. As he was walking back to his car he saw a woman waving at him from her front gate. As he looked up she started walking towards him. He waited.

"Hi, I'm Elaine. I just live a few doors up. There's nobody living there now. I suppose you know the old ....eh....well, the previous owner died. I found him you know. Myself and my husband. We rang the ambulance. Sorted it all out. Then his son from Canada comes over. Never gave his father the time of day up to this. Now he smells an inheritance and he over hot-foot. I mean I hate that, don't you? He takes over and never even thanks us for finding his father and keeping an eye on him over the years. All high and mighty, I'm living in Canada now, sort of attitude."

As she prattled on Greg felt like saying that he was his brother coming back from Australia to claim his share of the inheritance: but he didn't. To a policeman a gossip such as this was like gold. But like panning for gold you had to work through a lot of dirt to find the nuggets. But it was usually worthwhile. He eventually butted in.

"A woman with your local knowledge could probably help me".

He decided to go for broke.

"I work with the police and I am looking for some papers of Mr. ....eh .... Sims which may be of help in a particular case I am investigating."

Before Elaine told all the neighbours that Sims was a mass murderer he added quickly, before she could get a word in "it's nothing to do with him directly. He is not involved in any investigation."

She looked at him with obvious incredulity and might as well have shouted "I wasn't born yesterday" at him. Maybe he had misjudged the situation. If she started blabbing and word got back of a police investigation of Sims it wouldn't take them long to link it to Greg. He didn't think anything serious would happen to him; he was sure that they would gloss over it. But he would lose his chance of glory and for some reason that was now very important to him.

"In talking to you I am taking you into my confidence. You mustn't mention this to anyone else" he said, adding for effect "not even your husband."

Her eyes seemed to burn slightly brighter when he said this. Maybe she would beat the odds and keep her trap shut.

"Would you know where Mr. Sims' possessions might be now or who would have them?"

"Well I very much doubt if the son took much back to Canada. He seemed to find his father's house, and probably his possessions, distasteful. He looked at me as if I was mad when I implied he and his family would stay in his father's house while he was visiting. And it wasn't anything to do with finding the house spooky after his father dying there and all. No it simply wasn't good enough for himself and his wife. Snobs. They went into the house once after the funeral and stayed about 20 minutes. They must have left the house clearance to the estate agent's people. So I don't think he'll have taken much back. Bad and all as he thought the house was though, I'm sure he'll take the money from the sale."

Greg was relieved to hear that if there were any more notebooks, they were unlikely to be in Canada.

"So has the house been cleared yet to your knowledge?" he asked thinking that any house clearance operation would not have been below Elaine's radar.

"There was a large van there a few days ago but I'm not sure how much they took. He didn't seem to have much in his house when we went in and found him ... you know ... dead. So clearing the house wouldn't be a massive operation."

Greg felt he had got all he could from Elaine and so made to go.

"Now don't forget Mum's the word" Greg said as he started to get into his car. She smiled and mimed the action of zipping her mouth closed. As he drove away Greg wondered to himself how many people had wished that they could do that to her over the years.

CHAPTER 25

"I forgot to tell you to lock the car last night" Peta remarked to Peter as he walked into the kitchen to get himself some breakfast.

"What d'ya mean? We never lock the cars at night …. or the front door for that matter."

"It's just that I saw an old bloke out on the road when I drove off the other day. It's probably nothing but he looked like he was hiding behind the big tree. He looked a bit old to be casing the joint."

Peter felt slightly uncomfortable, but wasn't sure why.

"You're right. It's probably nothing. Probably one of the farm labourers eyeing a classy bird."

"You're such a sexist. You'll never change."

Peter laughed as he went upstairs for a shower. As he stood under the shower he recognized the uncomfortable feeling. It was similar to how he felt soon after Charlie's death. The police were always in and out of the house and he felt he was being watched all the time, although he never saw anyone and could never prove it. The memory of the stress of that episode made him go cold even though he was under a hot shower.

At that time he was still struggling with the business although he knew he was in for a large windfall from Charlie's estate. The nice people who lent him the money were not interested in the promise of their repayments in the future on the basis of some bequest. He was sure that the police, especially that O'Connor guy, had tried to slow down the solicitors settling up with him. They were hoping to pin the murder on him and as such Charlie's will would have been void. But they had failed and now he was rich. Still it was interesting that as soon as Peta had mentioned someone hanging around outside he was immediately reunited with those old feelings. It was like the smell of wet leaves transporting him back to the playground of his primary school. It was instantaneous and vivid. This was the same sensation. He knew that they would never pin anything on him. After a couple of years the investigation seemed to have settled down but Peter still wondered if the police were digging away out of sight and would suddenly confront him with a cut and dried case. He would wake up some mornings feeling happy and content and then he would remember that there was still Charlie's murder in the background and it would ruin his day. For a good while now (it was hard to remember how long it was because you didn't wake up one morning and say 'well that's that sorted' and get on with your life) he had relaxed and forgotten about the murder. He was shocked how easily he had been pushed back into that train of thought. It would never leave him he supposed. He was damaged, scarred, whatever: but hell, he was rich and enjoying himself.

He got out of the shower and as he dried himself he thought he might emigrate. Why not? He had thought about it before but refrained from action as he thought it might look suspicious. He wasn't one to worry about appearances but when it concerned murder he was as proud as the next man. He had decided to go to Spain. He knew he could be extradited back from there but he thought it would never come to that. He wasn't running away from justice. He just wanted to relax. He thought he had achieved that with his present position but when he realized how easily that peace could be destroyed he was rethinking the emigration idea. Would Peta buy it? He could run the business from abroad. He had good managers in place. He paid them well and they served him well. It was advice Charlie had given him. "Set up the business yourself and know every inch of it. Then bring a good manager in, show him the ropes, let him know you have an intimate knowledge of the business and how it is run, pay him well and leave him to it." It had been good advice. Charlie had been a smart cookie. If only ..... well it was no use having regrets now. His mind returned from the past to his emigration problem. The major downside was that Peta had a good private physiotherapy practice up and running and her involvement was very hands-on - literally. If she went abroad she would miss that. She was not the type of woman that would like to be "kept". Of course, she could set up in Spain, but that would mean starting over again. It was tricky. Anyway why was he going overboard about what was probably a farm labourer passing the house and feasting his eyes on Peta? It was one of the things he liked about going around with her: men always looked longingly at her and jealously at him. So why shouldn't some yokel have his share. He'd leave things alone for the moment. He was probably over-reacting. Things will look fine in a few days when his nerves calmed down a bit.

CHAPTER 26

Greg Harnett and Partners was the estate agent in charge of selling the old man's house. This was the name he had remembered plastered all over buses alongside an attractive woman saying "I'm moving in with Greg Harnett". The advertisement would certainly have put him off using him as an agent. He supposed old Sims hadn't much of a say in the decision of what estate agent to use. He pushed the door to open it despite the fact a notice on the door said PULL. He then pulled the door and, not surprisingly, it opened easily. A young, attractive woman sat at a reception desk. (Greg wondered fleetingly if she had moved in with Greg Harnett).

"Good morning sir. How may I help you?"

"Yes, good morning. I am interested in …well not actually interested in….I eh ….."

The smile was frozen on her face and her eyes were fixed on him. He was struggling like a fish on a hook. He used to be so good at this. The loss of an official capacity certainly led to a loss of confidence as well.

"Mmm, I want to enquire about the contents of a property you are selling. It's 3 Foundling Lane. Do you know it?"

"Yes, of course. What do you need to know about the contents?"

Greg decided not to use the police officer cover story here. Fooling Elaine was one thing but if his namesake Harnett got involved then things could get very awkward indeed.

"Mr Sims, the deceased owner of the property, sent me a note book before he died. I received it after his death. I have reason to believe that there are other similar notebooks and that Mr Sims would have wanted to show me these if he were still alive. That's why ....."

"I'll have to speak to Mr. Harnett about this. Have a seat and I'll be back to you in a minute."

She indicated a pair of chairs opposite her desk. Greg sat down and she disappeared through a door marked 'Staff Only'. He didn't foresee any problem in the estate agent co-operating. Hopefully he'd know where the notebooks were. They could be anywhere; he knew that. Maybe there were no others – that *would* be a right wild goose chase. He heard the door opening again and looked up. A rather overweight, bald man accompanied the receptionist. He was as white as a sheet and beads of sweat could be seen on his brow. He looked overwhelmed by life.

"This is Mr Harnett. He will be able to help you."

Greg found it hard to suppress a giggle. He didn't think his granny would want to move in with this bloke. What a cheek running that advertisement. Some people ..... Greg got down to business.

"Your … eh… colleague (Harnett looked cross), ….mmm…. assistant (seemed acceptable) may have mentioned to you the reason for my visit. I have reason to believe that the late Mr. Sims would have wanted me to have his gardening notebooks. He sent me one in the post just before he died but didn't tell me where the others were. I assume he would have given them to me if he had stayed alive."

Greg waited for a response.

"You're a keen gardener then" Harnett asked in a voice with surprisingly deep and silky tones.

"I'm sorry" Greg replied, being a bit slow on the uptake.

"The notebooks; do they have gardening tips? Is that why you want them?"

Now Greg understood.

"Oh yes, I love the garden. My late wife and I had built up a lovely garden over the years and it is still a great interest of mine."

There was no point in going into all the rigmarole about the murder etc. It might easily push Harnett over the edge.

"Well I appreciate your problem but you would have to take it up with Mr. Sims' solicitor. I could certainly give you his name."

"Could I ask you if you arranged to have the house cleared and if so did you find these notebooks?"

He hesitated for a moment and then turned towards the receptionist.

"Marian, did we have that house cleared?"

"Yeah, we got that chap Lindsay to do it after that other business with … you know …"

Her voice faded away without finishing the sentence. Harnett put on his cross face again. Some small scandal had raised its head. It didn't bother Greg. He had his own agenda to pursue.

"It would be good to know if they found the notebooks in the house. If I knew their location I could then approach the solicitor with a request to access them and even keep them if possible."

"I suppose we could give you the solicitor's number. It's a Mr. Hartson. After that it's up to you and him to sort things out."

Again he hesitated and you could almost hear the cogs turning in his head.

"Marian, give .... eh ..... this man Mr. Hartson's address and phone number, will you?"

He turned to Greg and gave him a weak smile and went back through the door into what was presumably his office.

Marian handed Greg a piece of paper with the contact details on it. She didn't bother with a smile. Greg nodded curtly, thanked her and left.

When he got on the street his mind was working overtime. Again his lack of official standing had left him powerless against Harnett. His bigger worry was that if he located the notebooks the solicitor would tell him to get lost. Would he then have to explain everything to Bill to get some official backing to twist the solicitor's arm? He'd have to wait and see.

CHAPTER 27

Peter was kicking himself. He'd been too smug. He had been basking in his wonderful life and had felt invulnerable. Now he thought things may be fraying at the edges. It was that peeping Tom that had sparked everything off. Despite all his rationalization Peter was still uneasy about the whole thing. His thoughts of emigration which he had had in the shower could not be shaken off even after a few days reflection. Peta was the problem. He knew it would upset her but he was fairly sure she'd come around to his way of thinking eventually. However her reaction to his suggestion of a move to Spain was much worse than he'd expected.

"I knew you'd come up with something like this. I just knew it. You're never happy with the quiet life, are you? Well I'm not going. I'm happy here with my life. I have built up my business and I'm not leaving it for anyone – not even you."

He could have questioned her motives for putting her business before him. But, if he was honest with himself, he couldn't be bothered arguing. It just hit him suddenly like that. If she didn't want to come with him, well bugger her. He wasn't going to beg. Surprisingly Peta began to try and compromise (well sort of).

"Why do you have to go? We're happy here and I am *really* happy with you. Why spoil it? What's the point? Do you not like being happy? Or have I been stupid and blind? Are you unhappy and this is one way of getting out of this relationship? Go on tell me. I want us to remain a couple. Do you?

'That's a lot of questions' Peter thought."

"I want us to stay together too but this move to Spain is something I must do. I can't explain. I just have to go."

She looked like she was going to cry but she pulled herself together and said in a bitter voice

"So you're choosing Spain over me. Thank you very much."

Peter thought he should have got in first with the "choosing one over the other" line. But as usual Peta had the upper moral ground.

"You'll have to trust me that I need to go. You remember all that stuff about the murder in the house. You know how that affected me back then. Well recently I've begun to feel jumpy again. For my own mental peace and ..... health – my mental health - I have to get out."

He looked at her and hoped for some understanding

"But that was ages ago. It was another life for you; you told me that yourself. There were your very words. Now you're...."

"Maybe I was fooling myself thinking I could get over such a thing so easily. It's obviously been fomenting at the back of my mind and now it's out again and I can't handle it very well.

He felt he might break down in tears but stopped himself. He then fleetingly wondered if tears might be the ideal method of persuading Peta to give in and accompany him to Spain. But no, he wouldn't do that because then she might come out of pity rather than because she wanted to. This would make for a very unhappy lady in Spain and that was the last thing he wanted.

"I am not becoming a psychological crutch for you Peter. You'll have to fight your demons yourself. I'm sorry."

They stared awkwardly at each other both realizing that what they had said over the last few minutes had ended their relationship. Neither of them knew what to say. Eventually Peta said in a very low voice

"I'll go. I'll come over tomorrow to get my stuff."

"Where will you stay tonight? Don't go if you've nowhere to stay."

"I'll stay with Marlene. She won't mind. She's still grateful to you for putting her up that time her apartment was flooded. So I'm sure she'll put me up to oblige you, if for no other reason."

"Well that's good" said Peter, looking a bit flustered. "Look you can really stay here if you want."

Peter remembered Marlene staying with him. It was around the time his business was going pear shaped. She was Peta's friend but Peta was having alterations done to her apartment and so Peter offered Marlene a room in his house. It was around the time that Peta and he had been chatting vaguely about moving in together. Peter always felt that Peta had felt Marlene had beaten her to it even though there were no suspicions or thoughts of any hanky-panky between Peter and Marlene by anyone involved. It just seemed not right to Peta; or that's how Peter saw it anyway. It seemed that Peta cooled about moving in for a while after that. Then there was the murder and Peta's move certainly dragged on longer that either of them envisaged. Anyway that was water under the bridge. He had more pressing problems now.

Peta seemed determined to leave tonight. Peter knew he should protest but he realized they both knew it would be a hollow one.

"Pop in anytime tomorrow. You have a key. You know, just …eh … work away" Peter said trying to sound magnanimous but feeling a lot less so.

"Thanks. Goodbye. I might see you tomorrow."

Peter nodded and thought briefly to himself that he would make a point of being out when she called. He then felt guilty about such thoughts. As Peta got into her car Peter's mind was filled with going to Spain. He felt he should do it as soon as possible now that Peta was out of the equation. As she drove off he went back into the house thinking about putting the house on the market. His soul mate was forgotten.

CHAPTER 28

G reg decided to go to a café and have a cup of coffee and a cake. He passed a few but they looked small and intimidating. Eventually he settled (as he usually did when he had a cup of coffee out of the house) on McDonalds. He liked the impersonality of the place and he could sit there and nobody paid him any attention. He had learned to bring a newspaper to read as he had got some peculiar looks in the past when he sat there looking around him. The place was always full of children and "looking around" always involved observing children. Well you couldn't be too careful these days – and so the newspaper. He told himself the apple tart was good and that was why he went there. But he knew that wasn't the reason. It was a safe place to go. Silly – he knew it was. He'd never tell the blokes in the pub that he went there for coffee. They would always be banging on about going here and going there for day trips and finding these quaint cafés that served fresh coffee with names Greg had never heard of. He pretended to look interested but was only fearful they would ask him to tell them about his favourite café. If he said McDonalds – so what? Well they would laugh at him, probably thinking he was joking. When they realized he was serious there would be an awkward silence. They would then pity him. That's why he never told people he went there. And his cronies would always meet *really* interesting people in these quaint cafés who would tell them their life story in 20 minutes and it would all sound so chummy (and they actually had stayed in the same hotel as us in Jo'berg) and Greg despised it. How could you get to know someone in 20 minutes? It was stupid and superficial. How could people waste their time with such talk. Sure, he spoke to the neighbours in the supermarket when they met and yes he liked this contact. But to talk to complete strangers, that was wrong. What fluff they talked about. Holidays, golf and golf courses and God knows what else. Utter nonsense. But a small corner of his mind was jealous. Jealous of the ease with which some people engaged in social intercourse. He could never think of what to say or worse still if he did manage to start a conversation he could never continue it. That was the worst. This is what kept him isolated. And isolated he was. He would mostly tell himself it was by choice but sometimes the truth would peep through – he would have preferred to be one of these pains in the neck rather than his tongue-tied self. Anyway he wasn't here to self-analyze. He was supposed to be preparing to meet the solicitor and find out about the other notebooks - if there were any. He knew it was a harmless request but because it was a strange one he thought it might make the solicitor a bit suspicious. Solicitors were suspicious people to begin with. By walking into their office they became wary of you; and that with no reason at all. A fishy request like Greg's was bound to sound alarm bells. He would go back home and get the envelope and the notebook. He could then show these to the solicitor and at least prove that he had had one of the notebooks sent to him by the Sims chap. It would do him no harm that the address on the envelope was to him at the police station. That would be a bonus he'd just thought of. Hopefully the solicitor (what was his name again, Greg thought) would probe his police credentials no further as Greg did not want to lie about being a policeman. If he went home now he could still make it back today with the notebook. He wanted to get it sorted out now, today. He never had any patience with this sort of thing. In his working life he would stay at his desk all night if it meant tracking down a lead. Until he had tied up a loose end he couldn't rest. Going home would mean tossing and turning all night in bed. So he'd work all night. He was praised for it by his seniors and colleagues. But he felt the praise was unjustified because it was in his nature. He couldn't avoid doing it any more than a bee could pass by a fragrant and colourful flower. He felt that old impatience back. It made him feel a little less vulnerable, a little less stupid, a bit more in control. He got up and left McDonalds and walked back to his car. He thought of paying a quick visit to Foster's place but as time was against him he decided to hold off that visit until another day; a day when he may have something significant to say to Mr. Foster.

CHAPTER 29

Marlene checked her phone as she left the ward. It had been on silent and she noticed she had three missed calls. She checked who the calls were from. They were all from the same caller – her friend Peta. Sensing something was wrong, but not knowing exactly why, she rang her back. She got the bones of the situation from Peta and was more than happy that Peta would stay with her while she got herself sorted out. Fortunately the spare room was made up and tidy. Her own bedroom was another matter. She was sad that Peter and Peta were having problems. She liked them both. Peter was a bit of a chancer but he was decent for all that. The more she saw of relationships she felt that men and women were not meant to live together for life. Women should live in communes. Some would be breadwinners others would tend to the children that some of the women would produce. The men could support the commune financially as well as supplying a fertilizing service for the women. It all sounded a bit futuristic but nowadays couples just didn't or couldn't stay together. The received wisdom was that couples stayed together for the children. Obviously this was not a factor with Peta and Peter. Her own experience of growing up with constantly rowing parents made her think that she would have preferred to grow up with one parent and a bit of peace and quiet. Herself and her sister were often the currency which was used to bargain during the rows. They had sometimes to pick sides. It wasn't much fun.

She started to tidy up the sitting room to make it look half decent for Peta's arrival. She couldn't help herself wondering how long Peta would stay. Maybe they'd get back together or if not Peta would be house hunting again. Marlene hoped it wouldn't take too long. She felt slightly guilty at wishing Peta out of her apartment before she had even arrived. But, well … she had her own life. She wondered what Dave would think. He'd probably feel Marlene was been taking for a ride. He was a nice guy but he looked after number one. Marlene was happy with that to some extent because it gave her some space and she liked that. Anyway she'd ring him and tell him what was happening and hope he wouldn't moan on and on about it.

'A key' she thought 'I'll need to get her a key'. She could ask Dave for his but that would not be a good move. Then he would have a moan-fest. She'd get one cut on the way home tomorrow. That should do. Peta usually worked late and as she was on an early shift tomorrow she'd be home first.

The next thing she thought of was wine and cigarettes. She would need plenty of both if they were to have a good soul-baring session tonight. She would pop down to the Spar shop now and be here when Peta arrived. She checked her purse and then with a quick look around to see if the place looked alright she went out the door to the shops.

CHAPTER 30

Peter had come back late in the evening. As he drove around the corner towards his house he saw that Peta's car was not there. That was a relief. He had stayed out late to avoid Peta when she came to collect her things. He hoped she had taken everything away as he didn't want to meet her again. They had had a good time but now that it was over Peter did not want to be in a position to have to go over old ground again and pick their relationship to bits. That was all a bit touchy/ feely to him. Nowadays you had to talk to someone to get over any traumatic experience. It wasn't his way. His philosophy was just get up and get on with it. The problem was that if you said you didn't want counseling then you would be labeled as someone who was suppressing the experience and so would be regarded as a pressure cooker waiting to explode at any time when the trauma of the experience finally hit you. So if you were in, say, the uniformed services you would be regarded as unreliable and could lose your job. Anyway Peter did not want to look back. He was looking forwards towards Spain and a better life. He had rented an apartment for a month. He reckoned he would see the lie of the land and then buy himself something. He was looking for a quick sale of his own house. That would help to stop him changing his mind and also free up some readies with which to purchase a property in Spain. He could have afforded to buy in Spain and keep his own home. But he felt that would give him an easy way back and he knew in the long-term that his peace of mind would be best protected if he broke all ties with the UK. He had taken the advice of a few accountants about tax, banking etc in relation to his business. He would keep things ticking over here for the moment but he might set up in Spain once he got a feel of the place. That would be ideal. For the moment he had complete faith in his managers and he would give them a hefty raise when he left for Spain. This should ensure their continued loyalty. He knew he should tidy up as the estate agent was sending a couple over the next day to show them around. He had decided that he could not show prospective buyers around himself as he loved the house too much. He almost felt he was betraying the house by selling it. Anyway he would tidy up in the morning as the agent had said he'd call in about 11.15 and the interested party would pop in about 11.30.

He went upstairs and checked the wardrobes and bathrooms and found that he was relieved (albeit with a small tinge of sadness) that all Peta's stuff was gone. He went to bed and slept soundly.

His alarm woke him at 9.30. He got up promptly and showered. He was surprised that he didn't feel lonely or even different now that Peta was gone. He was sure that he should feel ...... something. He was slightly disappointed that he didn't. Maybe his heart had turned to stone or maybe it was stone to begin with. He felt he was a hard, unfeeling bastard. At one time in his life he would have been proud to boast about that: but not now. He tidied up the place without much enthusiasm. He had a coffee while he waited on the agent's arrival. He wandered from room to room thinking about his times in the house. He loved it but as he walked around he could not conjure up any pleasant memories. He felt slightly annoyed. Surely he had had fun with Peta: but no, nothing specific came to mind. He had planned to walk around the house immersed in pleasant memories. He wanted to feel happy and cosy and warm in his memories. But that was not to be. A ring at the door made him jump.

"It's probably that bloody agent" Peter thought to himself.

He walked to the door gathering his thoughts.

"Ah, good morning Mr. Foster. And how are we today."

He was so bloody cheery. Peter felt himself very twitchy today. Maybe he was having some reaction to Peta's departure. Strangely that thought put him in better form.

"Yes come in. When is the buyer arriving?"

"About half-past. Boy, the place looks great."

Peter thought he looked confident.

The agent continued.

"I am very hopeful about this couple. They seem genuine and they would seem to have the financial means – as far as I can tell, that is. I know you should never judge a book by its cover and all that but, well ….. I have a certain experience in these matters. And as I said to you yesterday these houses are hard to sell. They are beyond most peoples' budget. But the Franklin's have been enquiring about properties out this way so when yours came up well it seemed to suit everybody so well. But I won't look too anxious to sell. I want you to get a top price. That's what I built my reputation on. Anyway we'll hope for the best."

Peter was relieved when he stopped talking.

"I think everything is in order" Peter said, mainly because he couldn't think of anything else.

"Mmm, I'll say" was the agent's response as he raised his eyebrows.

They both saw a car pulling up outside and the agent began to look nervous. The cockiness he had had minutes earlier had evaporated. He looked now as though he had possibly misplaced his confidence in the Franklin's. Peter signaled that he would make himself scarce in the garden and leave them to it.

In the garden Peter didn't hear the doorbell ring and assumed that the agent had got to the front door before the Franklin's had had time to ring the bell: so much for not looking too anxious to sell. Peter wandered around the garden and could occasionally see the threesome as they passed by a window. Lots of arm-waving was going and at one stage it looked like Mr. Franklin was standing on a chair inspecting one of the light fittings. After what seemed like hours (but in reality was only 20 minutes) Peter became inpatient and approached the house. He had intended to go in and "accidently" interrupt the showing of the house. As he came near the French doors leading from the patio into the sitting room the trio come out the side door. Peter could hear what they were saying.

"We had terrible trouble with the gutters in the last house and I'm not going through that again. I had to do it all myself. These workmen are hopeless."

"Oh darling, but you *love* fixing things" Mrs. Franklin said.

"Maybe, maybe, but I'm a busy man and haven't the time. Anyway these gutters look fine. Can't be too careful you know."

As they were returning to the house Mrs. Franklin asked "Did they ever get anyone for the murder that happened here?"

Peter froze. He waited for a reply but there was silence. He thought they had gone back into the house but after a long pause the agent said "What murder; here? I'd not heard."

"It was here, in this house wasn't it darling?"

"I think so. You know I'm not interested in that sort of thing."

And then to the agent "My wife loves crimes and crime dramas. I've had Morse and Midsommer Murders up to my neck."

Peter then heard the door shutting and silence returned.

"Damn" he thought "trust a woman to remember a murder."

He hoped that it wouldn't affect his ability to sell the place or indeed to get a reasonable price. He had changed his mind about running into the prospective buyers as he thought the murder of Charlie would dominate the conversation and he could do without that. He paced up and down the garden and soon the agent came out to find him. He was smiling and this cheered Peter up a bit.

"They love it. Particularly the wife or ..... partner or ..... whatever: she's very keen. She thinks there was a murder here for some reason and this seems to add to the attraction of the place. You meet all sorts in this line of work." He paused and then as an afterthought he asked a question in an incredulous tone of voice that implied he knew the answer.

"By the way was there *really* a murder here?"

"Yes" was all Peter said in reply.

The agent had started walking back up the garden expecting Peter to answer in the negative. When he heard the answer he turned around quickly his eyes alight with interest.

"You're serious, aren't you? Was this before you had the house? But no, I thought you bought it new."

Before the agent tied himself in knots with his thoughts Peter explained a friend of his had been staying while he was in France and had been murdered. Peter explained the memory was painful and was one of the reasons he was moving away and added that he'd rather not talk about it. The agent was clearly itching for more but in his favour he did not ask any more questions. Peter was sure he would be hotfoot to his computer to access Google to get more juicy information.

"So you think they'll put in an offer" said Peter getting back to selling the house.

"Pretty sure but at what level I don't know."

"Doesn't really matter. If it's in the general ballpark of the figure we spoke about just take it. I really want to move on."

"As your agent I'd have to advise you on the offer and inform you if I felt you could get more. I don't want you ....."

"Look, just do as I ask. I have my reasons. Money isn't everything to me. Not anymore, at any rate."

Peter could see the agent was backing off at least for the moment. As he would get 5% from the sale Peter could see the agent would be hoping for as high a price as possible. But he'd just have to do what Peter told him. Peter was employing him and Peter wanted to sell the house fast.

CHAPTER 31

Greg got home and headed straight to his sitting room and got the notebook. He thought of telephoning first but he had always found you got more attention by turning up at the door rather than ringing ahead. However those were the days when he actually was a policeman. They'd probably throw him out now but he was going ahead anyway.

He drove to town and parked around the corner from Hartson's office. He walked to the door of the office. It was a small affair. His was the only name on the door and it certainly wasn't a company with a list of partners' names as long as your arm. He opened the door and an old fashioned bell rang as he entered. It reminded him of the hardware store he used to go to as a child to buy candles or slug killer. There was no reception area as such and the area that you entered on coming through the door was one large room with two desks, many chairs scattered around and multiple filing cabinets covering all available wall space. In some places filing cabinets were on top of each other and looked extremely dangerous as well as difficult to access. It did not give one any sense of organisation but rather a feeling of a person struggling to stay afloat in a sea of chaos. The room was empty. Greg coughed and cleared his throat hoping to attract someone's attention but nothing happened. He hoped the filing cabinets did not contain confidential records as he could probably have made off with most of them by now (assuming the cabinets were not locked, which seemed unlikely). He was at a loss as to what to do next when a door at the back of the room (which he had not noticed previously) opened and an elderly man came through it coughing. When the coughing stopped Greg began to speak while at the same time the old man took off his glasses to wipe his eyes which were watering from the coughing fit. He heard Greg's voice and was visibly startled by it.

"Who's there? What do you want?" he said trying to quickly restore his glasses to their rightful place.

Greg thought this was a great start to his meeting with Hartson (assuming this was Mr. Hartson) but he also found the old man's reaction to his presence slightly strange. It was like he had broken into his house.

"Sorry to have startled you. I'm looking for Mr. Hartson."

"Who let you in anyway?" the old man asked as he started to focus on Greg.

"Nobody, the door was open. I just came in. I hope that was OK."

"She never locks the door you know. I think she's hoping someone will break in after office hours and murder me. There could be no other explanation for her constantly failing to lock the door."

He sighed and then looking around the room said, more to himself than Greg, "Now what did I come out here for?"

Greg thought it polite to wait for the old man to gather his thoughts before saying anything but when he noticed that he was about to go back through the door from which he had emerged Greg piped up "I'm looking for Mr Hartson. I just need a quick word."

The old man stopped in his tracks and turned around peering in the general direction of the voice before focussing on Greg again.

"Mr Hartson you say. Well that's me. But unfortunately as you see the office was locked up before you came in and I am officially finished for the day. Come back tomorrow if you like."

The man was obviously barmy and Greg felt that if he had taken the notebooks at some stage while settling up the gardener's affairs they could very well be in Timbuktu by now. He was about to back off and return the next day when he decided that he would use Hartson's slight derangement to his advantage.

"I'm actually here on police business and I just need to ask you a few questions about the estate of the late Mr. Frederick Sims."

'If he complains' Greg thought 'I can always deny that I said I was a police officer and he'll be too muddled to challenge me.'

Mr. Hartson smiled. "Always glad to help the police. What can I tell you?"

Greg saw a change in him. It was like the confusion had been an act. He hoped he had not messed up by mentioning police business.

"Can I confirm that you dealt with the estate of Mr Frederick Sims?"

"Well, yes. I have been, well, I suppose had been. But no, I suppose I still am his solicitor. Been it for years. There's nothing wrong, is there? It was me who pressurised him into making a will, you know" he added proudly as if he had been the person to give David Beckham his first pair of football boots.

"No his death is not a problem but before he died he sent me a notebook of his in which he kept track of his gardening tasks.

Greg took out the envelope and passed it over to Hartson. He looked at it briefly and handed it back. Greg hoped he had seen his name and that of the police station on the address on the envelope.

"He died before he could explain why he sent me the notebook. Suffice it to say that some of the observations in the notebook relate to a criminal investigation I am involved in."

Greg took out the notebook next and held it up.

In the course of dealing with Mr. Sims' estate have you ever come across a similar notebook or notebooks?"

"No. I can remember nothing like that."

"Of course they may have looked different: different sizes, different covers etc."

"No, nothing at all."

"Was there any gardening stuff at all with his belongings?"

"No. Of course he did all his gardening at the Crawfords'. Sure he'd no much garden at his own house."

'Of course' thought Greg 'he had been stupid. Not match fit, as they say. The bloody notebooks would be up at the Crawfords' place. That's where he would have written in them each day and where he would have referred to them.'

Greg brought the interview to a quick end and thanked Mr. Hartson for being so helpful.

"Maybe you better lock the door after me" Greg said as he turned to leave.

"Lorna should do that when she leaves" was all he said and returned through the door from which he had first emerged.

Greg shrugged his shoulders and thought that Hartson was as mad as he had first appeared. Thank God for that.

CHAPTER 32

Peter got off the phone. He wondered if he was being screwed. Spanish property agents made British second hand car dealers look like Office of Fair Trading employees. Even though he had only been on the phone to his agent he felt like checking to make sure that his wallet and watch were still on his person. The guy had sounded nice enough on the phone but time was not on Peter's side and the agent picked up on that. Money was not a problem but it went against the grain to be screwed in a business deal.

His house was as good as sold. The Franklins had put in a reasonable offer and, fighting off protests from his estate agent, Peter had accepted it. Once the paperwork was done the sale should be through within two weeks: the sooner the better. He had started to pack up his stuff and had contacted a removal company that would bring his belongings to Spain. The nearer the move came the more anxious he became. He had a feeling that he was never going to get a chance to get to

Spain. There was no logical reason for this. It was real paranoia and so unlike him. The packing seemed to encourage him that the move would really happen and so he kept going.

As he pressed ahead with his mindless packing he took the luxury of fantasising about life in Spain. If his businesses here kept growing money wouldn't be a problem. That was his greatest comfort. He thought he might lease or even buy a boat and spend his days fishing. He would become a local expert and people would come to him for advice about local fishing. He would spend the nights in a local bar beside the marina. He might have a woman there as well. They could live separately and have their own independence. Ok, she might want them to move in together but, hey, that'd be fine. Then she'd move out when they had a disagreement. 'I think I better think it out again' came to Peter's mind.

Or maybe he would remain unattached and play golf and, who knows, if he got his handicap right down he might play for money. The fact that he had never played golf in his life did not seem to deter such thoughts. Or maybe he'd become a gambler: all day in bed and all night in the casino. But no, he thought, that'll end in ruin.

These things were running through his head when the doorbell rang. He went down to answer it. It was the estate agent.

"We're go, go, go" he said, eyes bulging like a bull-frog with excitement.

This guy had been recommended to Peter as an experienced agent. To Peter he was like a rookie. He'd certainly sold the place quickly but that had been his good luck that the Franklins were interested rather than a first class sales pitch. The other good thing about the Franklins' interest was the lack of the need for advertising and so there was no public knowledge of his plans to emigrate. The local gossips would have their noses out of joint at missing out on this juicy news.

"Do I have to do anything?" was all Peter could muster.

"Just sign a few things and move out by the 23rd."

"Sounds do-able."

The agent put his brief case on the coffee table in the large hall and clicked it open with great self-importance. He shuffled some papers and then produced a few sheets that he laid on the table.

"Just sign here, here and .....eh.....here" he said pointing at some Xs with his pen.

Peter got his own pen and signed as requested. The papers were gathered up again making maximum noise, replaced in the brief case and the clasps were snapped closed with great aplomb.

"A pleasure doing business with you Mr. Foster. I'll send the bill in the next 24 hours and I would be grateful if you could settle the account before you leave for Spain."

'He's changed his tune' Peter thought. He suddenly looked and sounded like the professional Peter had been led to believe he was. They shook hands and Peter stayed at the door until the agent had driven away.

'Well that's done now' he thought 'no going back'. He knew he should be happy that it was sorted out and in one way he was. On the other hand he felt deep down that he was being driven from his home. But he was certain that his peace of mind was dependant on this move and that's why he wasn't turning back.

He looked out the window as he passed through to the kitchen. A slightly battered beige Ford Fiesta was driving up the small road Peter's house shared with his two neighbours' houses. He hoped it wasn't calling to him. He did not wish to speak to anybody. He just wanted to be gone far away and the sooner the better.

CHAPTER 33

Greg had left the solicitor's office annoyed with himself that he hadn't thought to look for the other notebooks at the Crawford's place. He had lost his edge. Anyway even if he recovered more of the notebooks it still may not amount to anything. It was probably a wild goose chase. But the fact that Sims had intended to deliver to him personally at the police station a notebook, presumably knowing that he was the chief investigating officer of the Osgood murder, must mean something. Unless Sims was in a similar position to himself: bugger all to do and all day to do it. Then he might have been thinking any rubbish in order to justify giving him the notebook. Still it was worth pursuing to the end.

He drove out to the Crawford's house. It was a lovely day and it felt good to be out of the city. Driving this route gave him a good feeling. He felt like he was an active detective again. Many times he had driven this road before hoping against hope that he could trip up Foster. He had always returned with his tail between his legs. But here he was again – on Foster's trail. He drove up the driveway which the Crawfords shared with Foster and someone else. He thought that the other house had changed hands a few times since he had been carrying out his investigation and he had no idea who lived there now. The Fiesta's tyres crunched on the stones as Greg parked on the driveway at the side of the house. He got out and walked slowly to the front door looking around him to see if he could spot Crawford in his garden. All was quiet. He went to the front door and rang the bell. It was one of those fancy chimes that played a tune. He remembered the tune from those years ago when he came to interview Crawford after the murder and he still couldn't put a name on it. He wondered if Crawford would remember him. He hadn't long to wait because at that moment the door was opened by Crawford who immediately greeted him by his name and previous title.

Greg did not enlighten him about his retirement from the force but took the proffered hand and shook it.

"Come in, come in. How have you been?"

As Greg entered the house at Crawford's beckoning he looked back at Foster's house. He wondered whether he was in or not. Then he realised Crawford was still talking.

"Are you still investigating the .... eh .... crime next door? I suppose you boys never let it rest until you have someone, eh?"

He winked at Greg in a conspiratorial fashion but Greg just smiled back in a non-committal way.

"You're right" said Greg, feeding Crawford's ego "I'm still looking for answers."

Greg had relaxed a bit because he did not think there would

be any problem with Crawford co-operating as he clearly thought Greg was visiting in an official capacity.

"This may seem a strange request but I need to ask you about Sims, the gardener who used to work for you."

"Ah yes. That was a sad day indeed, very sad, very unfortunate" Franklin said.

"You mean about his death" Greg asked.

"Oh yes, that too, of course. But, no, the day he left me was a terrible day. He was an excellent gardener. I've had no one decent since he left. They are either ponces with degrees in horticulture who wouldn't get their hands dirty if you paid them. Or else they are labourers who dig your garden all day but wouldn't know a rose from a tulip. Do you know what I mean?"

Greg nodded to be pleasant but never having employed a gardener or indeed any domestic help he was not in a position to know what Crawford meant.

"Mr Sims was about to visit me or deliver to me in the police station a notebook which was mainly concerned with his gardening chores. Did you know he kept such a notebook?"

Crawford looked genuinely puzzled by the question as if Greg was testing his general knowledge rather than asking him to recall a personal memory.

"I'm afraid I don't really know anything about that. He was a quiet man and kept himself to himself. You know he visited me here the day before he died." He paused wondering what else he could say.

"He's not in any trouble himself" Greg started to say but then realised how foolish that sounded. He tried another tack.

"I know you wouldn't want to blacken Mr. Sims' memory in

any way and you won't. He is suspected of no wrongdoing but may have noted some incident in these notebooks that might help me with the case."

"But you said they concerned his chores. How could they be relevant to the .... eh .... case?" He winked at Greg again.

Greg tried to butter him up as bit more. "Between you and me he made some observations about .... well, your neighbour and one of these might have some relevance. I think Mr. Sims recognised the relevance himself and was coming to tell me about it. But he died before he met me."

"There was nothing suspicious about his death, was there?" Crawford asked with mild terror in his eyes thinking he might be next on a hit list.

"No, not at all: perfectly natural."

There was silence then and Greg wasn't sure how to proceed. They both felt slightly awkward but Crawford broke the silence first.

"I'm not sure how I can be of further help."

Greg felt a door closing in front of him. He had no other leads to follow. That was the end of this little adventure. Back to the twice daily supermarket visits for him. A thought flashed into his head.

"Could I look around his .... well, potting shed, or wherever he did his bits and pieces in the garden. There might be something there."

"Of course, but I've been doing some work there on and off over the last few years and have not seen anything. Also some of the so-called gardeners were in and out of there,"

Greg was led through the house and out the back door. A cat was sitting on the step and got up and stretched as they passed. There was a little wooden shed at the bottom of the garden under an old oak tree. It had originally been painted green but most of the green paint had peeled away leaving the bare wood exposed. Greg thought that Sims would not have let it get into that state.

"Well here it is."

He opened the door which stuck a bit.

"Sims used to keep it locked all the time. Of course in his day there was a lot of valuable stuff in here. Not anymore though."

It looked like a dumping ground to Greg and if he was to find another notebook he'd have his work cut out for him. Should he abandon the whole thing or get stuck in and look through this junk: if Crawford would let him, that is. But then he realised Crawford still thought he was acting in an official capacity and so was unlikely to turn him down, although he might smell a rat if he did all the searching himself rather than get some uniformed help involved. He decided to go ahead with the search and not worry what Crawford thought.

"I am afraid we'll have to search this shed as part of the investigation" Greg announced as officiously as possible.

"Oh, I don't mind. Maybe you could tidy it up as you go" Crawford responded in a dejected voice. "Just carry on when your help arrives. I'm going out."

Greg was pleased with this turn of events. He went back to his car by going around the house and hoped Crawford would think he was summoning help. By the sound of his last answer he didn't care.

After about ten minutes Crawford came out and got into his car. He waved at Greg as he drove passed. Greg waited for about five minutes and then got out of the car and returned to the shed. He thought he should have probably gone home and changed into old clothes. He was going to be a mess after this, but he didn't want to miss the opportunity of Crawford being away from the house.

Over the next two hours he moved lawn mowers, wheel barrows, pots of all sizes and shapes, garden implements the purpose of some of which he could not imagine. There seemed to be at least two of everything and the deeper he went the older and dirtier the stuff became. He didn't want to stop for a break as he hoped to be away by the time Crawford got back. When he had cleared everything out there was no notebooks to be found. The walls were solid as were the shelves and there was no secret compartment to hide anything. Not that Sims would have wanted to hide his notebooks: why should he?

Originally Greg had planned to put all the stuff back in some order and tidy up the place as Crawford had requested (?tongue-in-cheek). However he was tired out and disappointed and wanted to get away. He flung the stuff back in no order and although he felt bad he told himself it wasn't his job to do Crawford's tidying up. He walked up around the side of the house to go back to the car. He saw the glasshouse and wondered if there was any chance the notebooks might be there. The inside looked tidy and certainly wasn't messed up by the presence of any plant life. It was obvious that since Sims had retired the garden had lost an excellent carer. The glasshouse had loads of empty pots in various states of disrepair. Greg slid the door open and put his head inside. It was warm and smelt musty. There was a row of shelves against the far wall. There were two drawers on the floor level. Greg picked his way over through the pots. The drawers were difficult to open.

The first drawer contained lots of different types of twine knotted around each other. Greg opened the second drawer in a dismissive fashion, expecting to find nothing. When he looked in he did a double take. Inside were some old fashioned school copy books with orange covers. They did not resemble the notebook that Greg had in his possession but they were more hopeful than the twine. Greg lifted them carefully out. Why hadn't he checked here in the first place?

The books each had a year on the cover. Greg opened the one for 1998 and sure enough inside was the spidery handwriting that he had seen in the other notebook.

March 8 Daffs starting to show. Must bring pots to front of house in the next week or two. Primroses still looking good. Will cut them ......

Greg skipped to July.

July 13 Plums looking really good. Need more thinning.

Onto September.

Sept 30 Dahlias very strong with vivid colours. Must use the Roster feeding on them again next year.

There was nothing about Foster. Maybe he hadn't noticed Foster at that time. He then looked in the 1999 copybook and began to read it. January, February, March: nothing above and beyond gardening. In April Greg noticed a footnote in the style of the references to Foster in the original notebook. It was April 21st.

That bloody fellow next door nearly knocked me down in his car as he turned into the drive. I have a good mind to report him to the police. He didn't even acknowledge me. He's a right bloody Smarty Pants.

'So that's where the initials come from' thought Greg.

CHAPTER 34

Peter Foster was relieved when the Fiesta drove to the Crawfords' house. He saw an old man getting out and walking up to ring the door bell. Crawford opened the door and seemed to know the man as he appeared to have invited him in immediately. As the old man was entering the house he looked over at Foster's place. Peter visibly flinched. He knew the old man. It was .... eh .... that policeman. What was his name? Connell? No, O' something. O'Connor, that was it. What the hell was he doing here? Maybe it was just a social call. He might be a friend of Crawford for all he knew. Despite these weak attempts at reassurance he felt his heart racing and sweat breaking out on his upper lip. He wished he could go and get on the plane right now. He felt claustrophobic. He kept staring at Crawford's front door as if trying, by sheer force of will, to keep O'Connor inside the house. Eventually he tore himself away from the window. He thought about going for a long drive and coming back late or maybe even booking into a hotel overnight to try and avoid O'Connor. Then he thought he would feel better keeping an eye on events across the road. 'Roll on next week' was the carrot that kept him going.

He needed something to occupy him. He thought of the attic. He had remembered it the other day and needed to check if it was empty. He had a vague recollection of putting some stuff up there. He got a ladder and opened the hatch. There were a few boxes and he spent the next couple of hours getting them down and sorting through the stuff. When he was finished he realised he had relaxed a bit but as soon as he realised it he felt the anxiety creep up on him again. He went to the window at once and noticed with some relief that Crawford's car was gone. His relief was short lived when he saw O'Connor's car was still parked at the side of the house. Now what was going on? Why was O'Connor still there when Crawford was gone? He stood very still. Was he being watched? He had an urge to throw himself flat on the floor but felt stupid for thinking like that. He was concerned that his nerves were so raw. He couldn't see the cocky and confident Peter Foster he knew and loved so well.

He moved away from the window and pressed himself up against the wall so as not to be visible to anyone looking in from outside. After a few minutes he peeped out the window to see if he could see O'Connor. Nothing moved. It was deadly quiet. He decided to go to the back of the house and see if the policeman was lurking around there trying to spy on him. He felt silly creeping around his own house but he was genuinely spooked. As he made his way to the upstairs windows at the back he thought he remembered hearing that O'Connor had retired from the force. Maybe that was duff information but by the look of him he should be well retired. If he was no longer with the police then any business here would be unofficial, unless ..... he couldn't think of an "unless". These thoughts didn't make him feel any easier in himself. He wondered if O'Connor was the guy that Peta had seen snooping about the place. He was sure it must have been him.

When he got to the back window he peeped out but again saw nothing. Where the hell was he? No wait, maybe he went off with Crawford. That must be it. They went off in Crawford's car and that's why O'Connor's car was still outside. With this reassurance of sorts Foster decided to look around his own garden and outhouses. He went out the back door and had a good look around the garden. There was nothing. He checked the garden shed and then went around the front to check the garage. As he emerged at the front of the house his mobile phone rang and he fumbled to get it out of his pocket. As he did so it fell on the grass. As he bent down to pick it up he noticed a movement in Crawford's garden. He looked up briefly and saw the old man coming around the side of the house to the front. He also noticed Crawford must have returned when he had been around the back. They obviously hadn't gone out together. Crawford noticed O'Connor and went to greet him. Peter ducked into his garage and didn't think either of the men had seen him. By now his phone had rung-out and when he looked at caller ID it was Mrs. Franklin. She probably wanted to come and measure another room. He decided not to return the call.

CHAPTER 35

Greg wondered if he should take the notebooks or leave them and ask permission from Crawford at a later date. As Crawford thought he was still in the force he probably wouldn't mind if he took them. As he was walking out of the glass house he heard a car pulling up. As he rounded the corner of the house he saw that Crawford had returned. He decided he would tell Crawford that he was taking the notebooks and would return them when he had finished with them. He hailed him.

"Mr. Crawford, I was just leaving. I'm taking these notebooks of Mr Sims' and I'll return them when I've finished with them."

"Well you found what you wanted then" Crawford replied looking pleased. Greg was happy that no complaint would be made to the police about him taking the notebooks. Suddenly from somewhere the sound of classical music was heard. Greg looked quizzically at Crawford.

"It's his nibs' phone" he said nodding his head in the direction of Foster's house.

"It's certainly loud enough" Greg said, squinting his eyes to show his displeasure. He looked over at Foster's house but could see no sign of life. As suddenly as it started the music stopped. Greg let out a sigh of relief.

"It's terrible to see such lovely music played in such a tinny way" Crawford said with regret in his voice.

"What's the piece anyway" Greg enquired.

"It's John McCormack singing Macushla. If I'm not mistaken it's a Victor recording from New York City in 1911. Sims loved the piece, you know. I have the recording in my collection. So does Foster by the sound of it."

Greg vaguely remembered that Sims' notebook had mentioned that recording as Foster's ring tone previously. Foster must love the piece himself if he had kept the same ring tone on his phone for all those years. With these thoughts in his head he bid farewell to Crawford and made his way back to his car. He was looking forward to getting home and reading the notebooks and hopefully finding out what Sims wanted to tell him.

He stopped at the local corner shop and got a small sliced pan and two tomatoes. He decided to have tomato sandwiches for his tea. He really wasn't hungry but he thought he'd feel sick if he didn't eat something. He was fairly confident he would find the solution to the problem in the recovered notebooks but he told himself he'd have his tea first and then start looking through the notebooks in detail. In one way the delay prolonged the anticipation of the eventual solution (as he hoped). It also put off the possibility of failure which was in a small corner of his mind. He didn't consciously think in terms of failure but it would intermittently dart in and out of his mind like a fly in a room that you only notice when it buzzes in your ear.

He made a pot of tea as he planned a long evening before he went to bed. He hoped to go to bed with the issue resolved. He turned on the evening news while he had his meal. He wasn't concentrating on what the newsreader was saying but the noise was comforting. When he had finished his food he washed the dishes slowly and deliberately. He tidied up the kitchen a bit and threw out some old newspapers. When he couldn't find anything else to do he sat down with all the note-books and started with the 1995 one.

CHAPTER 36

Peter was annoyed with himself. Why had he become such a wimp? His guts were in a knot with anxiety. He longed for Spain and peace of mind. This was intolerable. It was seeing O'Connor that had really spooked him. Those years ago he had handled O'Conner and anyone else they threw at him with consummate ease: not any more. Only two days to go. He had drawn all the curtains in the house and was sitting in the dark and in silence like some weirdo. He felt he was being watched but was too scared to look out and see if anybody was there. He had thought of going to a hotel for the next two nights but he had to be at the house tomorrow to direct the movers. He poured himself a single malt Scotch. Normally he would have savoured the flavour and quality but now he was simply hoping that the alcohol would relax him. He might as well have been drinking methylated spirits for all he tasted. After a few minutes he felt the alcohol kicking in and poured himself another. If this is what it took to get through the next few days then so be it.

In one way he thought the present situation assured him he had made the correct decision in moving to Spain. When Peta had refused to go and had left him he wondered about the wisdom of his actions. But now there was no mistake. He had to go and go quickly. It was his divorce from Helen that started all this. If only things had worked out between them. If only he hadn't played away. If only he could have resisted his urges. The next girl he met was always someone special. There was always the irresistible attraction, the animal magnetism and the fate that brought them together. You couldn't fight your destiny. But the attraction soon paled and the hassle of trying to keep two women happy became too much ... until the next time. It was only after the divorce that he settled down to a stable relationship with Peta. And now that was over. Looking back he could never see what attracted him to the women in his life: all except Helen. He still regretted losing her. It was hard to put into words but since he had broken up with Helen he had always felt a bit of him was missing. If he'd stayed with Helen he probably wouldn't be hiding in the house with the curtains drawn. He smiled to himself when he thought how invincible he'd felt when Helen had divorced him. He didn't need anyone. He was his own man and he certainly didn't need any woman to keep him happy and fulfilled. He'd be fine. How wrong he had been and it had taken him a few years to find that out. But sitting here wishing time away he knew he had made a mistake. And it was only now, with hindsight, that he could appreciate the size of that mistake.

He began to relive some of the good times with Helen and was almost in a trance as he lost himself in fond memories.

The sound of the letterbox brought him back to reality. He immediately became tense and anxious again as he wondered who was at the door. He crept silently on his hands and knees out into the hall and over to the porch door. He peered through the glass porch door and saw somebody had put a leaflet through his letter box. He crawled into the porch and retrieved the leaflet. He wondered if it might be as note from O'Connor or even Crawford but it was just a circular from some retired local bloke offering his services as a gardener at very competitive prices. Peter threw it back on the floor. Well he might as well go to bed: at least he'd be comfortable and warm there.

He crawled around the house and made sure it was secure and the burglar alarm was set. He finally found his feet and walked up stairs. He comforted himself that this was his second last night in the house and after tomorrow night he would be in Spain and free.

'Just hang in there me ol' cocker' he told himself, 'just hang in there.'

CHAPTER 37

G reg was tired and could hardly keep his eyes open. He
was also very disappointed. He had gone through the
diaries from 1995 to 2003 when Sims had retired. He had read
lots of gardening tips and lore and when to do what etc., but
there were few other references to Foster. It mentioned his
flashy showing off of his wealth both before he lost everything
and after he became wealthy again. But there was nothing
here to help him as a policeman (retired) solve the case. It
was the only reason that he could think of as to why Sims
was going to send him or more likely bring him the notebook.
Why else bother? But it told him nothing. He had gone over
it again and again. Nothing. He felt empty and let down.
What had he wasted the last few weeks for? What was Sims
up to? He probably was a mad old man with nothing better to
do than waste police time with his fantasies. If only he could
have spoken to Sims. But that was a futile avenue of thought.
He hoped Bill wouldn't ask him why he wanted the old Osgood

murder files. He'd fob him off again. Even though it seemed like a dead end he wasn't going to admit to anyone what a wild goose chase he'd been led on by Sims. If the old guy was alive he'd strangle him. He began to tidy away all the notebooks with the intention of going to bed. He picked up the original notebook and flicked through it, reading bits and pieces.

As soon as he saw it he knew he was right. Of course, he should have realised it. He was getting sloppy. He'd need to see Crawford again or at least telephone him. He looked at his watch. 'God almighty' he thought to himself 'it's two in the morning.' He'd have to ring Crawford tomorrow. His innate impatience kicked in and he knew that if he was still on the force he would have called Crawford and damn the consequences. However as he lacked official approval he thought he'd wait until morning, even though Crawford still thought he was active on the force. Sleep was out of the question. What would he do tomorrow if and when he confirmed his suspicions? Would he confront Foster or tell Bill his suspicions and let him handle it. He didn't know. He'd wait and see how things went. He put on the kettle and made himself a cup a coffee. He didn't know why he'd made it. He certainly didn't need caffeine to stay awake. It was just something to do. He paced the floor. He put on the radio and turned it off again after a few minutes. He looked over at the television but decided against turning it on. Eventually he sat on the armchair and fell asleep. He woke up with a fright but immediately knew that he needed to ring Crawford and why. He looked at his watch. It was coming up to 7.30. He'd wait until 8 o'clock. He put on the kettle but couldn't face a cup of tea. His stomach was in a knot. It was a familiar feeling from a previous life: the one he got when he felt he was on the verge of breaking a case. He must have looked at his watch 100 times between 7.30 and 8 o'clock. At last it was time to ring. He hoped he'd be there.

"Hello."

"Hello, Mr. Crawford. It's Greg O'Connor here, from the police. I was with you yesterday."

"Mr O'Connor. You're on the go early. I suppose you policemen never get a rest. Crime never sleeps and all that."

"Yes, quite. Can I ask you something?"

"Fire away."

"You told me yesterday that the day before he died Mr. Sims visited you at your home. Can you tell me if he heard Foster's phone ringing while he was there with you."

"You policemen surely ask strange questions, but yes he did. The reason I remember is Sims' reaction to it. We were standing at the front door talking. When he heard Foster's phone ringing he stopped talking to me and seemed to be somewhere else. He then bade me a short and vague farewell and went around the back of the house. I didn't know what he was doing so I just went back into the house to finish writing a letter I was composing when he called. I assume he left and went home eventually. The next thing I heard was that he had been found dead. It was a shock, you know, particularly after seeing him so soon before his death."

"Thank you very much Mr. Crawford. That's a great help. I won't disturb you any longer. Good-bye."

Greg's hand was shaking as he hung up the phone. He had cracked it or at least he hoped so. He also now understood Sims' reason for planning to see him and bring him the notebook.

He felt good. There was life in the old dog yet.

CHAPTER 38

Peter Foster was waiting impatiently for the movers. The hall was full of boxes. It was hard to get in and out without falling over the boxes. As he walked around his footsteps echoed loudly on the wooden floors. He was staying at the airport hotel tonight and would be away first thing in the morning. He looked out again but of the movers there was no sign. He looked at his watch. It was 8.45. They said they'd be there by 9.30 so there was time yet. As he turned away from the window he noticed a Ford Fiesta driving up the wee road between Crawford's house and his. It looked like O'Connor's car. What the hell was he doing back? Crawford and he were certainly best mates these days. He watched as the car turned into his drive. 'He must be turning' Peter thought, but felt his guts tighten when the car stopped and O'Connor got out and made his way to the front door. Foster's immediate thought was to prevent O'Connor seeing that he was moving. He mustn't let him into the house. Then he thought of the movers. Up until now he was wishing they would come but with this unexpected change of events he was hoping they'd delay until O'Connor had gone. He'd get rid of him quickly. What business had O'Connor with him anyway? He ran to the door and opened it and went outside and shut it again as if he were leaving the house. He tried to look surprised when he saw O'Connor but he wasn't sure how well he'd pulled it off.

"Hello Mr. Foster. Long time no see, as they say."

"You're that detective that interviewed me a few years ago about poor old Charlie Osgood's murder. Do you have any news?"

Foster was surprising himself at how he was handling the situation. He'd pretended he had forgotten O'Connor's name. He'd just need to play it cool and hopefully get rid of him in a few minutes.

"I have some news as a matter of fact. I was sure you'd be interested so I came all the way out here to tell you."

"Have you found the nurse then?"

"Yes I have actually."

Peter was startled by this news and he could see that O'Connor had picked it up.

"Well pray tell who is she and where is she?"

"She, or should it be he, is standing in front of me. You were the nurse and you killed Mr. Osgood. I always thought it but now I know it."

"I don't have good enough legs for a nurse and according to those who saw her it was a female nurse. You're talking rubbish."

Foster was again impressed at his own coolness.

"You flew to Spain and flew straight back again under some alias. You then dressed up as nurse and killed Mr. Osgood.

You then flew back to Spain under the alias and carried on your walking holiday or whatever. You certainly made a point of turning up at your hotel on the day you were supposed to return from your trek across the Pyrenees. I am not sure of the details but that's the bones of it."

"You sound like a crazy man. You must be going senile. How dare you accuse me of murdering my best friend and supporter. You should leave."

"The support he gave you after his death was much more than he gave you when he was alive. Aren't you curious to know why I know you murdered Mr. Osgood?"

"I couldn't care less. It's the ramblings of a feeble mind. Where are your colleagues? Do any of them share your ravings? Now that I come to think of it you're retired. You're not here on official business at all. You're pursuing your own vendetta against me. I think I'll call the police and have you removed. What do you think of that?"

"Your phone and the nurse's had the same unusual ring tone. So you either gave her a loan of your phone or you were the nurse. I think it was the latter. I know it won't stand up in court but I'll get more evidence and return here to arrest you. Mark my words, I will."

"I'm serious, get out or I'll call the police."

Greg turned on his heels and returned to his car. He drove slowly out the drive and then turned right and headed back to town. About half a mile down the road he had to pull in to let a large removal van pass. He hardly noticed it and when it passed he pulled out and headed back home.

CHAPTER 39

So he knew. That old bugger. He knew. Foster felt he'd kept his head and he knew that O'Connor had nothing concrete on him. Still it was a bit scary. But he was getting out and O'Connor seemed to have no idea of this. He had the key in the door to open it when he heard the removal van pulling into his driveway. He realised he cut it fine enough and was grateful that O'Connor hadn't stayed another minute. The driver got out and gave him a wave. Foster gave him the thumbs up and the driver beckoned to his assistant. They joined Foster at the front door. He had met the driver before when he came to give him an estimate of the moving costs. The key would be given to the Franklins tomorrow and that would be that. He would go to Spain with no worries. He had his health. He had plenty of money and he was sure he'd meet someone special or maybe he'd meet loads of special people. That might be more attractive. Only time would tell.

O'Connor was a tenacious so-and-so. How had he linked

up the phone ring tone? It was a stupid mistake. Of course it was. But how had he found out about it? Thinking about it made Foster feel jittery. It was like O'Connor had some special powers. But he knew that was stupid. But after all this time what had happened to bring this information to light. Foster assumed that it must have only come to light recently or O'Connor would have paid him a visit before now. It must be linked to his visit to Crawford yesterday. But knowing O'Connor he would have come across last night if he had found out anything useful. He had paid some late night and early morning calls to Foster when the case was in its early stages. In some ways he admired O'Connor for the way he dedicated himself to a cause. Even now as a retired policeman he was still pursuing the matter. It was for no other reward than personal pride. Foster could respect that in O'Connor but he himself would have needed some more tangible reward for his efforts. Foster knew he'd won. There had been a war between them over the years. It had eased off recently but today's battle was probably the decisive and final one. He began to feel sorry for O'Connor. 'My God' he thought 'I'm definitely getting soft. What the hell is happening to me? Maybe it's the thought of emigration. It must be affecting me emotionally.'

But deep down he knew that O'Connor's dedication to a cause made him almost jealous. Here was a retired guy who was still chasing his prey to the end. And for what? His car was twelve years old. A policeman's pension was probably a pittance. Foster knew he'd got away with it and he was the criminal. O'Connor for all his doggedness was left with nothing, not even the certainty of Foster's guilt. Life certainly wasn't fair.

He went into the house to see if he could help the movers

but quickly realised he was just in the way. He went out and sat in the garden and lost himself in thought.

"That's us done Sir."

Foster jumped.

"Great, thanks."

He took a £50.00 tip from his pocket and gave it to the driver.

"Very kind Sir. Hope all goes well with the move. We'll see you on the other side."

Foster thought the £50.00 was money well spent. It would guarantee good service from the movers down in Spain.

The movers van reversed carefully out of the drive. Foster did a quick check around the house. It was empty. He felt there was no point in delaying any longer so he locked up and drove into town to the solicitors. He gave the house key to the receptionist who put it in an envelope and wrote the address on it. Foster smiled and walked out onto the high street. He headed for the bank and emerged from there after about half an hour, his business completed. He then went into Clinton cards and made a purchase. His third stop was the post office. After this he drove to the hotel at the airport where he was to spend the night. An acquaintance would collect his car in the following few days and keep in storage for a while until he was convinced he would be staying in Spain long-term. After the events of the last couple of days he was sure he would not be returning very often.

He checked into the hotel and went to his room. He could gradually feel the weight coming off his shoulders. With each passing minute he was getting closer and closer to his final escape.

CHAPTER 40

G reg had been in limbo for the last few days. He wanted to do more to try and nail Foster. But he didn't know how to proceed. It was a cold case and to start such an investigation was a difficult thing. Generally it required new information coming to light (the mobile phone in this case – but it was not very solid evidence from a forensic point of view) and then a lot of man power to resurrect and question all the original witnesses. By himself it was a non-starter. His original thoughts had centred on doing this solo and getting all the credit for himself. Now he saw it was hopeless and he was doomed to failure unless he sought help. But would Bill think he was mad? All he had was the ramblings of an old gardener and his own evidence of hearing Foster's phone ringing. Not exactly a smoking gun. He didn't know what to do.

He heard the postman put his post through the letter box. He always felt obliged to go and get the post immediately. He didn't know why as it comprised circulars, bills and credit card offers. He picked it up off the floor. There was a bank statement, an offer to give him the perfect lawn in three months and another white envelope which looked like a birthday card. It wasn't his birthday for months and anyway nobody sent him a card anymore. His interested was piqued.

He went back into the kitchen and sat at the table. He found a knife on the table and slit open the envelope. He took out a card thinking it was a mistake and it was not for him.

"Happy retirement" he read on the front.

He opened it and a piece of paper fell out. He picked it up off the floor. It was a cashier's cheque for £25,000. His heart beat faster. What was going on? He then read what was written on the card.

"To a retired policeman from a retired nurse. Best wishes."

'Not signed' he thought 'but he's admitted it, more or less. Was that enough? Did he need to be punished as well. And the money: should he keep it?'

He sat for a long time with these thought buzzing back and forth across his brain. Eventually he stood up and decided to have lunch and then go shopping for his tea. And you know what, he might even go to the pictures tomorrow.